FACE OFF

What Reviewers Say About
PJ Trebelhorn's Work

Twice in a Lifetime

"*Twice in a Lifetime* is a sweet and easy read with two likable characters whom readers will root for. Featuring a widow and a police officer who share the same tragedy, the book deals with their intertwining backstory tenderly and thoughtfully. *Twice in a Lifetime* also features a compelling antagonist, a welcome dash of action and great explorations of power dynamics within lesbian relationships."—*RT Book Reviews*

The Right Kind of Wrong

"[A] nice, gentle read with some great secondary characters, easy pacing, and a pleasant writing style. Something you could happily read on a lazy Sunday afternoon."—*Rainbow Book Reviews*

"PJ Trebelhorn has written a romantic, sexy story with just the right amount of angst."—*Kitty Kat's Book Review Blog*

"Quinn has had her heart broken in the past and to avoid it happening again decides to enjoy life as a player. She's always had feelings for her best friend Grace but when they met they decided to be friends and Quinn will always honor that commitment. Grace however is only now realizing twenty years later that she has maybe had feelings for Quinn all along…but can she take a chance on them losing their very close friendship? The love story between these two characters is well formed and you can understand their feelings for one another as well as knowing the inner turmoil of potentially losing your best friend. …"—*Les Rêveur*

Taking a Gamble

"This is a truly superb feel-good novel. Ms Trebelhorn is obviously an accomplished writer of engaging and riveting tales. Not only is this a very readable novel but it is full of humour and convincing, beautifully written and conceived realities about falling in love for the first time."—*Inked Rainbow Reads*

Desperate Measures

"I love kick-ass police detectives especially when they're women. This book contains a superior specimen of the breed."—*Rainbow Book Reviews*

From This Moment On

"*From This Moment On* is a fine read for coping with loss as well as being a touching lesbian romance tale."—*Midwest Book Review*

"...Trebelhorn created characters for *From This Moment On* that are flawed, faulted and wholly realistic: While many of the characters are struggling with loss, their unique approaches to dealing with it reveal their weaknesses and give the reader a deeper appreciation of the characters...*From This Moment On*... tells a gripping, emotional story about love, loss and the fusion of the two."—*Philadelphia Gay News*

Visit us at www.boldstrokesbooks.com

By the Author

FACE OFF

by

PJ Trebelhorn

2019

FACE OFF

ISBN 13: 978-1-63555-480-9

THIS TRADE PAPERBACK ORIGINAL IS PUBLISHED BY
BOLD STROKES BOOKS, INC.
P.O. BOX 249
VALLEY FALLS, NY 12185

FIRST EDITION: DECEMBER 2019

CREDITS
EDITOR: CINDY CRESAP
PRODUCTION DESIGN: SUSAN RAMUNDO
COVER DESIGN BY MELODY POND

Acknowledgments

Even after this, my eleventh book, I remain in awe that I've been so lucky to be a part of the Bold Strokes family. My eternal thanks goes out to Radclyffe, Sandy Lowe, and everyone else who works in the background to make things run so seamlessly.

Thank you to my editor, Cindy Cresap, who makes the editing process virtually painless. You're a rock star!

I also have to thank my sister, Carol; my chosen family, Susan and Harvey Campbell; and my wife, Cheryl. Your support means the world to me, and I thank you all.

But most of all I thank you, the readers, who make all of this possible. Thank you for the notes via Facebook and email to let me know you've enjoyed my books. As long as you keep reading, I'll keep writing.

Dedication

For Cheryl, always

CHAPTER ONE

S avannah Wells loved her job. Both of them, actually. By day, she was a veterinarian, but at night, she was living her dream as a semiprofessional ice hockey player. The designation of "semipro" was simply because she was a woman. She had no doubt if she was a man, she'd be at least in the minor leagues. Hockey had been her one true love for as long as she could remember. Her parents nurtured that love, and she knew she'd never be able to thank them enough for all their support.

Of course, that didn't stop them from trying to come up with ways for her to thank them.

"When are you going to get married and give us grandchildren?" her mother Lisa asked one Saturday afternoon in late June when Savannah came over for their weekly lunch date. Sometimes it was brunch, but usually just lunch.

"I'm not," Savannah replied with a shake of her head. Long-term in regard to relationships had never been on Savannah's radar. Maybe someday, if the right woman came along, but she really didn't see it happening anytime soon. Mostly because she wasn't even looking. In fact, she was actively *not* looking.

"Why are you so cynical when it comes to love?" her other mother, Faith, asked from her seat across from Savannah as she took another spoonful of potato salad from the bowl in the center of the table.

"I don't know. Why are you both so adamant about me getting married?" Savannah tried to sound serious, but they knew she was teasing them, as this was the standard conversation whenever they got together. Not a week went by without them asking about the state of her love life. Or lack thereof, as was the case.

"Come on, Vanna," Faith said with a smirk, knowing how much she hated the nickname. It always made her think of Vanna White.

"We just want you to be as miserable as we are." Lisa chuckled as she blew a kiss to Faith.

"You two make me miserable enough as it is," Savannah said. "Who needs a wife when I already have two women nagging the hell out of me all the time?"

Savannah smiled at them, enjoying the easy way they were with each other. While it was true her moms had only been legally married for four years, they'd been living together for over three decades. They met three years before Savannah was born. Savannah always hoped she'd one day find the kind of love her moms had. So far, at least, that hadn't worked out so well.

"I think your mother has another blind date for you," Faith said with a wink before shoving a forkful of potato salad into her mouth.

"No," Savannah said, shaking her head adamantly. Lisa was looking at her with the pleading expression she'd seemed to have perfected over the years. Savannah shook her head again, but never broke eye contact. "Just…no. I don't need help finding dates."

"You're never going to meet a girl to settle down with in those clubs you go to," Lisa said.

"I'm not looking for anyone to settle down with, and need I remind you that you guys met in a club like the one I go to?"

"First of all, I don't think the clubs back then were anything like they are now," Faith said. "And second, there weren't a whole lot of options for meeting other lesbians back then."

"Okay, I understand that," Savannah said in her way of conceding the point. "But I really don't like blind dates. At all. Seriously."

"What could it hurt?" Lisa held a hand up to stop Savannah from answering right away. "How could meeting new people possibly be a bad thing?"

"Do I really need to point out the blind date disasters you've set me up on in the past?" Savannah tried not to laugh when Faith snorted and covered her mouth. Lisa just stared at her for a moment before motioning for her to go ahead. Savannah sighed and leaned back in her chair. "What about the one who wanted to move in with me the same night we met? No, actually a mere *ten minutes* after we met. She insisted we'd known each other in a former life and were destined to be together."

"Or the one who was a mime?" Faith laughed, and Savannah couldn't help but join her. Lisa simply stared at them both with her arms crossed over her chest.

"Oh, my God, she showed up wearing her mime makeup and clothes and wouldn't say a word the entire evening," Savannah said, doubling over in her chair.

"And let's not forget Chris," Faith said, wiping tears from her eyes.

"Okay, that one wasn't funny." Savannah sobered quickly and shook her head.

"It kinda was," Faith said. "Maybe not at the time, but it is now. Admit it."

Savannah shook her head but snorted with the effort of trying to keep her expression neutral, because yeah, since some time had passed, it was funny. Kind of.

"You two are hilarious," Lisa said, still looking as serious as could be, which caused even more laughter.

"Lisa, Chris was a guy," Savannah pointed out. "I still don't get how that happened."

"It was a misunderstanding." Lisa was smiling now too, and Savannah pressed a hand to her side because it was starting to hurt from laughing so hard. "She was talking to me about her daughter, and then she said Chris would probably love to meet you. How did I know my boss was suddenly referring to her son?"

"Thank God he was a good sport about it," Savannah said with a chuckle. "I could go on—"

"And on, and on," Faith added.

"And on," Savannah said with a nod. "But I don't think I can handle any more laughing today. Just please, stop, Lisa."

Some of Savannah's friends thought it was odd for her to call her moms by their first names, but it had been their idea from the beginning. They said it helped to avoid any unnecessary confusion for all of them, so she'd always addressed them by name.

"Fine, I know when I'm not wanted." Lisa stood and carried her empty plate into the kitchen. Savannah started to stand in order to go after her, but Faith placed a hand on her forearm and shook her head.

"I need to tell her we were just teasing her," Savannah said.

"She knows, honey." Faith had more gray hair than brown now, but she still didn't look a day over fifty, even though she was knocking on sixty's door. She nodded once and released her hold on Savannah's arm. "Lisa's a master of manipulation. You should realize that by now. She knows you'll feel bad for hurting her feelings and you'll run right out there after her. Just let her be for a minute, and she'll be back."

Sure enough, less than a full sixty seconds later, Lisa rejoined them at the table, and began eating again.

"Are you two done making fun of me?" she asked after a few moments of silence.

"No one's making fun of you, Lisa," Faith said, covering her hand with her own. "We were simply pointing out how your blind date attempts for our daughter haven't really worked out too well in the past. You can admit that's true, right?"

"No," Lisa said, but it was apparent to Savannah she was trying hard not to smile. Savannah watched her for a moment until Lisa finally started to laugh. "The mime was pretty damn funny."

"You know what wasn't so funny though? The stalker chick. It took months to get rid of her, and you promised after that one you'd stop." Savannah looked between the two of them, all mirth disappearing from the table. She hoped they would remember the fear they all felt when the woman refused to take no for an answer. Savannah had actually worried she would break into her house one night while she was sleeping and murder her. She'd even gone as far as to spend most nights at Lisa and Faith's house.

She'd been convinced that particular incident would have been enough for Lisa to stop trying to set her up, but it seemed as though she was going right back to doing it on a weekly basis, if not more often. Savannah was getting dangerously close to her breaking point. She was sure Faith knew it, but Lisa was a little hard headed when it came to wanting Savannah to find a relationship that would last.

They finished eating and Savannah helped clean the kitchen before she finally decided it was time to get home. Her cat, named Leo because he looked so much like a lion when he was a kitten, would be mad at her for being gone so long, as he always was. When the team went on a road trip, he came and stayed with his grandmas and was spoiled rotten.

"Your brother and his wife are coming for the Fourth," Faith said as they walked her to the front door. "Should we expect you?"

"And a date, perhaps?" Lisa added with a hopeful tone.

"The team has to be at the carnival for most of the afternoon, but I'll be here after it. Just don't count on a date," Savannah said with a slight chuckle and a roll of her eyes only Faith could see since she was hugging Lisa good-bye at the time. "Would it be okay if I invited Lori Abbott and her kids?"

"Court's sister? Absolutely," Lisa said as she released her. "She's always welcome here."

"I sometimes think you'd prefer Court as your daughter over me." Savannah smiled at what had been a running joke between them for years.

"When is her wedding?" Faith asked.

"July twenty-eighth," Savannah answered. "That way they can go on their honeymoon and be back to Chicago in time for Court to be at training camp. And before you ask, they'll be here a week before the actual date so they can tie up any loose ends in the planning department."

"I hope you're planning a hell of a bachelor party for her," Faith said with a wink.

"Not me," Savannah said. "Gail is standing up for her, so it's on her."

Savannah, along with her own best friend, Kelly Rawlins, were Court's line mates on the Kingsville Warriors for more than five years and had become good friends with her on and off the ice, but Court's best friend had been Gail Crawford, the Warriors' head coach, for the better part of twenty years. Truth be told, it didn't bother Savannah one bit that Court had asked Gail to stand with her at the wedding. As far as she was concerned, it was too much pressure to make sure everything went right. All she had to do was show up and have a good time.

"Kelly's coming over this afternoon, so I have to get going," Savannah said.

"Kelly's a nice young woman," Lisa said, and Savannah banged her forehead on the door a couple of times. "I'm just saying."

"She is a nice young woman, Lisa," Savannah said. "But she's like a sister to me. You know that. It is never going to happen."

"You can't say I didn't try."

Savannah heard this last bit as she pulled the front door closed behind her. She knew she was lucky to have parents who supported her in everything she did in life, but Lisa really needed to keep her matchmaking ambitions to herself.

CHAPTER TWO

"Damn, Van," Kelly Rawlins said from where she was standing by the front window. "Have you seen your new neighbor? Yummy."

Savannah walked over to stand next to her and gazed out the window to the house next door. All she could see were guys at the moment, so she bumped her shoulder into Kelly's and smiled.

"You aren't switching teams on me, are you? Because I only see an ungodly amount of testosterone over there."

"You know me better than that," Kelly said with a laugh. "I'm pretty sure they're all professional movers. I'm hoping the one woman I saw is moving in there alone. She's enough to give you wet dreams for a month of Sundays."

"Yeah? Get the hell out of my way." Savannah shoved her aside and then laughed at Kelly's look of indignation. She shook her head and walked back toward the kitchen. She'd known the house had sold, but Gail, the seller's Realtor, hadn't given her the heads-up about whether or not it was a single woman—lesbian or not—who'd bought the place. It didn't matter though. "I don't care how hot or not she is, she's off limits to both of us. You know the rules."

"Yeah, yeah, but I'm telling you, once you see her, you'll be willing to bend the rules." Kelly planted herself on a stool at the breakfast bar and watched Savannah as she finished putting the chicken breasts she was grilling later in the marinade.

"Don't count on it," Savannah said as she put the container in the refrigerator and grabbed a couple of beers before going to join her at the bar. "I won't get involved with a neighbor, or anyone else who knows where I live for that matter. It opens me up to all kinds of messy and uncomfortable scenarios."

"Yeah, but I don't live here." Kelly winked and took a long draw from her beer bottle.

"And *you* don't date my neighbors either."

"That was never part of the rules."

"It was never an issue before. Now it's part of the rules."

"You're no fun."

"I've heard quite a different story from the women I meet." Savannah grinned and took a drink of her own beer. She and Kelly had been friends since grade school, and they came out to each other shortly before starting high school. That was when Kelly had come to live with them after her parents had been killed in a car accident. Since they were the only two lesbians either of them knew of, it made sense for them to date each other, right? They never got any further than kissing, and maybe a couple of groping sessions, but soon realized they were much better as friends. They'd been inseparable ever since.

"I'm sure you have."

Leo jumped up on the counter and came over to rub on Savannah's hand. She scratched behind his ears and he started purring loudly before flopping onto his side then rolling onto his back so she could rub his belly.

"So spoiled." Kelly shook her head.

"Rotten," Savannah said.

"All right, I've got to run a few errands," Kelly said as she finished her beer and got to her feet. "I'll be back for dinner though, and we're still going to Allentown tonight, right?"

"Absolutely." Savannah gave Leo a kiss on the end of his nose before following her to the door. "Call first though, you know, in case the new neighbor drops by."

"You really are an ass sometimes," Kelly said, shoving her middle finger in Savannah's face.

"Careful where you put that finger," Savannah said with a laugh. "I may be a hockey player, but I do still have all my teeth."

"You might not when I get through with you." Kelly blew her a kiss before turning and going down the front walk to her car in the driveway. "Love you, Van."

"Love you too, Kel," she said. Savannah stood on the front porch for a few moments pretending to watch Kelly, but she was really hoping to catch a glimpse of the new neighbor. After Kelly drove away, she gave up and went back inside. "What do you think, Leo? Is your aunt Kelly yanking my chain? The neighbor's probably eighty years old, isn't she?"

Leo meowed and wove his way between her legs, almost tripping her in the process. She reached down and picked him up, and he immediately began to purr.

"Let's take a nap, little guy, otherwise your Aunt Kelly isn't going to be happy when I fall asleep in the car on the way to the dance club."

❖

It was after four when she woke up to someone knocking on the front door. It was too early for Kelly to be back, so she wondered who it could be as she forced Leo off her chest and sat up on the couch. She stood and rubbed her eyes while she walked to the door.

"Hi." That was what she wanted to say when she saw the woman standing on her front porch, but all she could do was stare. If this was the new neighbor, she was definitely not eighty years old.

"Hello," the woman said as she glanced over her shoulder toward the house next door as if she were nervous to be standing there. When she met her eyes, Savannah almost gasped, but somehow managed to smile at her.

"Can I help you?"

"Yeah, my name is Madison Scott, and I just moved in next door," she said with a smile that threatened to turn Savannah into a puddle. Madison shifted her weight and chuckled as she shook her head. "I really can't believe I'm standing here asking you this, but I was wondering if I could use your shower. Please."

Savannah wasn't sure what she'd been expecting to hear, but that certainly wasn't it. She cocked her head to the side and looked out at the street. This had to be a joke, right? Some hidden camera show? Maybe Kelly had put her up to this.

"Um, I've never been in the house you bought, but I'm pretty sure it has indoor plumbing." Savannah grinned at the blush spreading across Madison's cheeks. "Did you forget to have the water turned on or something?"

"No, there's water. The utility company seems to have forgotten I needed the gas turned on yesterday though." She ran a hand through her short blond hair before shoving her hands in the pockets of her shorts. "While I'm not opposed to taking a cold shower when the need arises, I'm really not in the mood for one today."

Savannah stepped aside and motioned for her to come in. Leo, being the love hog he was, immediately ran over and began checking out the new person in his house. He stood on his back legs and placed his front feet on Madison's thigh.

"Leo, stop," Savannah said, but Madison was smiling when she bent over to scratch him under the chin.

"Can I pick him up?" she asked.

"You can, but if you do, you might have to take him home with you."

"I'm not sure my dog would like me bringing home a cat."

"No worries on that front," Savannah said. "Leo would whip him into shape in no time."

It was infinitely easier to talk to Madison when she wasn't looking at Savannah. When she didn't have to see the beautiful green eyes and the perfectly crooked smile Madison gave so freely and which caused Savannah's heart rate to increase. What the hell was going on with her? Madison was more athletic and less feminine than the women she was usually attracted to. But anyone would have to be blind to not see how gorgeous she was.

"He doesn't mind dogs?" Madison asked as she stood up with Leo looking as though he were in heaven cradled in her arms. Savannah experienced a small stab of jealousy at the sight.

"He thinks he's a dog most of the time." She felt silly standing there near the front door, and thought maybe she should offer her guest a drink. But then she remembered why Madison was there in the first place. "The bathroom is at the end of the hall. Extra towels are in the cupboard by the sink, and there's plenty of shampoo and conditioner, if you need it."

"Thank you so much," Madison said with one of those heart melting smiles. "I'm going to dinner at my sister's house tonight, and I've been sweating my ass off all day. But hey, I'm moved in. It'll take me forever to get unpacked, but at least it's all there."

"Did you need clothes too?" Savannah asked, noticing for the first time she hadn't brought anything with her to the door. "I'm sure I could find something for you to wear, but they'd be a little big, I think."

Savannah took the opportunity to allow her eyes to roam Madison's body. They were close to the same height, but it was pretty obvious she had more muscle and bulk than Madison. Which certainly wasn't a bad thing, she thought as her eyes stopped momentarily on her chest.

"You're a naughty one, aren't you?" Madison said, causing Savannah to jerk as she looked at her face, fearing she'd been caught checking her out. She breathed a sigh of relief when she saw Madison was actually talking to Leo, who was nipping at and then licking the tip of her nose. Madison met her eyes and winked at her. "He's a lover."

"Yes, he is." *So am I.*

"I feel like I'm asking too much of you already," Madison said, moving toward the couch so Leo could jump out of her arms.

"I can run back home and try to find the boxes with my clothes in them."

"What are neighbors for, if not to offer a hot shower and clean clothes?" Savannah asked with a shrug.

"You're a life saver, and I'd hug you if I weren't so sweaty." Madison said, looking relieved. "I'll only be a few minutes."

"Madison," she said when she headed toward the bathroom. She wanted to tell her she didn't mind a little sweat, but thought better of it. The woman was probably straight, and a comment like that would only cause problems. "I'll leave the clothes on the chair outside of the bathroom."

"Thanks, and please, call me Maddie." She blew her a kiss, and Savannah was sure she was going to hyperventilate.

After she got the clothes for her, and fought the temptation to actually take them into the bathroom, knowing there was an incredibly gorgeous—and naked—woman in her shower, she walked quickly into the kitchen and grabbed a beer from the fridge. Leo was on the counter watching her, a self-satisfied smug look on his face.

"You, sir, are a whore," she told him, and she laughed when his tail swished in response. "But, dude, she blew me a kiss. Do straight women do that to another woman they just met?"

He meowed and just stared at her. She shook her head.

"You're right, little man," she said, setting her bottle down and running a hand through her hair. "I never even introduced myself. What a freaking idiot I am."

A few minutes later, the bathroom door opened, and then Maddie came walking down the hall toward the kitchen. She was smiling and finger combing her wet hair as she sighed, sounding to Savannah like she was extremely happy to be clean.

"Is this your name on the back?" she asked, indicating the Warriors jersey Savannah had given her to wear. Savannah nodded. "Is there a first name to go with it? I don't usually use a woman's shower without at least knowing her name."

"Savannah," she said, the reference to using a woman's shower not escaping her notice. She filed it away for future reference. Maybe she was off base with the assumption Madison was straight.

"So, you play hockey?"

"I do."

"I don't know much about the game, really. I'm more of a baseball fan."

"I won't hold it against you." Savannah grinned and offered her a beer, which Maddie declined.

"I should really be going," she said, looking disappointed. "I still need to find my clothes so I can make it to my sister's before dinner. I'll get these back to you tomorrow, if that's all right?"

"There's no hurry," Savannah said, walking her to the door. "Besides, I know where you live."

"Yes, you do." Maddie stopped before walking out and turned to hug her. Savannah froze at first, but then hugged her back. She couldn't suppress the shiver running through her when Maddie spoke softly into her ear. "Thank you for the shower, Savannah Wells. I'll see you soon."

Savannah found she couldn't speak, but she simply nodded when Maddie released her and then turned to leave. She stood there for a moment to regain her composure, then realized Kelly would probably be there any minute. She needed to get the chicken on the grill.

Chapter Three

Maddie decided to wear the jersey Savannah had loaned her to her sister's house for dinner. It was comfortable, and it smelled like Savannah. Holy crap, was she beautiful. Maddie felt as if she'd won the next-door neighbor lottery, and she couldn't be happier. It was going to be a wonderful summer if she was going to have a front row seat to Savannah wearing shorts the entire season. Her legs were amazing, both powerful and muscular. Unlike her own, which were toned enough thanks to her being a part-time jogger, but they certainly weren't as drool-worthy as Savannah's.

She'd spent more time than she normally would have fawning all over the cat because she was captivated by the eyes that were such a light color of blue they appeared to be gray. And she'd seen in them what she was sure Savannah had been trying to hide—desire. She couldn't suppress the smile as she glanced at herself in the rearview mirror. The hug certainly hadn't been planned, but she'd needed to know if the rest of Savannah's body was as fit as her legs. It most definitely was.

Her heart was beating faster than normal as she pulled into her sister's driveway. She shut the engine off and sat there for a few moments, hoping her thoughts wouldn't be written all over her face for Dana and her family to see. The front door opened and she saw her fourteen-year-old niece leaning against the frame watching her. After a deep breath in an attempt to calm herself, she got out of the car and headed toward her.

"Oh, my God!" Amy screamed as she ran toward her. Maddie stopped as her niece slowly circled her, wondering if she had some incredibly large bug on her shoulder or something. "Please tell me this isn't an authentic game worn jersey because I may have to steal it from you."

"I honestly don't know if it is or not," Maddie said, looking down at the front of it. She shrugged. "It wouldn't surprise me if it was though. But it isn't mine, so you can't steal it."

"What the hell is going on out here?" Trent, her incredibly handsome brother-in-law, asked as he appeared in the doorway. "Jesus, Amy, the way you screamed, I though you must have been abducted by aliens or trolls or something similarly hideous."

"Dad, look at what she's wearing!" Amy said.

"Let's take it inside," Trent said with a small smile. "I think you're scaring your aunt."

"Just a little," Maddie said with a wink, holding her thumb and forefinger close together.

She followed them into the house, smiling at the energy Amy wasn't able to contain. Maddie watched as Amy ran straight to the kitchen and came back out, dragging Dana along behind her. Maddie removed her shoes, because her sister always insisted on it. Yes, she was one of *those* people, just like their mother.

"Look, Mom!" Amy yelled, pointing at Maddie. "Look at what she has on!"

"It has to be a Savannah Wells jersey, or else you wouldn't be this excited," Dana said, shaking her head. She met Maddie's eyes and smirked. "When did you become a hockey fan?"

"I'm not, really," Maddie said, although she was seriously beginning to think she needed to become one. She hugged her sister, even though they'd seen each other just that morning when she'd picked Trent up in order to use his muscle to help move her furniture into the new house.

"It *is* game worn," Amy said, obviously in awe as she grabbed the sleeve and inspected it.

"How can you tell?"

"There's black marks on it from the puck." She looked at Maddie and scowled. "Where did you get it?"

"Funny, that," Maddie said with a grin. "My new next-door neighbor has the same name. She let me borrow this when I had to use her shower this afternoon because the gas company didn't turn on my gas."

"Shut. Up." Amy stared at her in disbelief. "You bought the house next door to Savannah Wells?"

"I did."

"I am so spending the night at your house as often as I can," Amy said, looking at her mother. "Like every weekend."

"I think you need to work that out with your aunt." Dana sighed and shook her head at Trent. Maddie couldn't help but snicker at the entire scene. "Maybe she doesn't want you around all the time."

"Are you kidding?" Maddie asked as they all made their way to the kitchen. "My standing as the cool aunt just skyrocketed. I wouldn't want to risk losing points now."

"You might change your mind when you realize she means it," Trent said as he snatched a carrot stick out of a bowl on the counter. "She has a little bit of a crush on Savannah Wells."

"Dad," Amy said, making the word sound as though it had four syllables. She hung her head and walked out of the room.

"How do you guys even know who she is?" Maddie asked, suddenly curious.

"The Kingsville Warriors are the hottest ticket in town," Dana said, pulling a pan out of the oven. Maddie's stomach growled at the divine aroma from the roasted chicken. "They're the closest thing we have to a professional sports team unless you want to travel to Allentown or Scranton."

"And those places have baseball, right? Minor leagues?" Maddie asked.

"And minor league hockey too," Trent said. He pulled plates out of the cupboard and began setting the table. "There are a lot of kids around here who love the Warriors. Of course, there were a lot of them who were very disappointed when Courtney Abbott was traded away. She was a bit of a local celebrity."

"Courtney Abbott? She was a teammate of Savannah's?"

"Don't tell me you know her too," Dana said.

"Actually, I do."

"Oh, God," Trent said, rolling his eyes. "You've just been elevated to coolest aunt *ever*!"

"How do you know Courtney?" Dana asked before yelling for Amy to join them for dinner.

"Actually, I know her fiancée, Lana Caruso. They're getting married here next month," Maddie said as they took their seats at the table. "They've hired me to photograph the wedding for them. Why is Courtney Abbott a local celebrity?"

"Two Olympic medals for ice hockey, is that reason enough?" Trent asked.

"Yep, I would say it's more than reason enough." Maddie took a deep breath and shook her head. It was settled. She was going to have to study up and learn everything she possibly could about ice hockey. Especially if she hoped to be spending more time with Savannah. And she absolutely was.

"You could do worse than Savannah Wells," Trent said, and Maddie laughed. "What?"

"I just met her today. You sound like you expect us to be married tomorrow."

"I'm just saying," Trent said with a shrug and a look to Dana that Maddie knew was a plea for help.

"You're on your own with this one, honey," she told him. "Maybe next time you should just keep your mouth shut."

"Keep his mouth shut about what?" Amy asked as she flopped down in the chair across from Maddie. She pointed at Trent and laughed. "You're in trouble."

"I'm not in trouble," he grumbled good-naturedly. "I just need to learn to think before I speak."

They kept conversation to more mundane, and safer, subjects while they ate, and Amy retreated to her room after she'd cleared the table and loaded the dishwasher. Apparently, the fact Maddie knew Savannah had lost a bit of its shine. It was just as well because she really didn't want to think about her any more than she already had since leaving her house earlier.

"So, I can't believe you actually asked her if you could use her shower," Dana said after Trent went to his home office to get some work done.

"I know, right? Even more amazing is she let me," Maddie answered, resigning herself to the fact she wasn't being given an option as to whether or not she was going to think—or talk—about Savannah.

"Right?" Dana laughed. "Is there any kind of a spark there?"

"Dana, I spent about five minutes with her."

"She's not attractive?"

Maddie snorted, and immediately regretted the reaction. Dana grabbed her arm and gave it a squeeze, causing Maddie to roll her eyes. Her sister was so much like their mother, always wanting to talk everything to death, and not giving up until they had every bit of detail they could possibly get.

"Since your daughter is so enamored with her, I'm sure you know what she looks like," Maddie said. She extricated herself from the grip Dana had on her and rubbed her arm. "So I have to wonder why you're asking a question you no doubt already know the answer to."

"Yes, but I look at women differently than you do."

"God, Dana, you make it sound like I want to sleep with every woman I see."

"Oh, stop, you know what I mean." Dana sighed in obvious exasperation, and Maddie smiled. She loved teasing her. "I might think a woman is attractive, and you could have absolutely zero interest. On the other hand, you might fall head over heels for someone I don't find attractive at all. Like Mary."

"Okay, stop," Maddie said, all humor gone now. Why the hell did she have to bring up Maddie's ex?

"When are you going to talk about it, Mads?" Dana asked, looking all concerned while she used her childhood nickname. Maddie shook her head. "Jesus, she is the reason you moved here in the first place, right?"

"Yes, to get away from her. To forget about her. To *move on*."

"I get it, I really do," Dana said, sounding sincere. But how could that be when she kept pushing Maddie for the details of their breakup? "I just think in order to truly move on, you need to get it all out of your own head. I'm on your side, sweetie. I want to help."

"She was verbally abusive," Maddie said, even though she really didn't want to talk about it. She knew Dana was right though—she probably needed to talk to someone about it. And actually, now that she'd said it, she wondered why she hadn't opened up about it sooner. "And possessive. *Way* too possessive. I couldn't have friends, and God forbid if I ever went somewhere without her. She was convinced I wanted to sleep with any woman I happened to speak to. Ironic, isn't it? It took me finding out she was cheating on me to finally end it."

"Oh, sweetie, why didn't you ever confide in me about this?" Dana moved closer and held her hand. "You know you can talk to me about anything, right?"

"I was embarrassed, Dana," she said, shaking her head. "I couldn't believe I'd put up with it for so long."

"Hey," Dana said with a quick squeeze to get Maddie to look at her. "I'm your sister. You don't have to be embarrassed about anything, okay? Promise me you'll talk to me if anything like that ever happens again."

"I will, but I think maybe you should just shoot me if I'm stupid enough to get involved with someone like her again." Maddie let out a humorless chuckle. "I'm sorry I didn't come to you."

"I'm so happy you got away from her." Dana hugged her tightly and then backed away so she could look her in the eye. "I would have gone after her myself if I'd known what she was putting you through. Although Trent would likely have beat me to it."

"I know this about both of you," Maddie said with a sad smile. "And I love you for it."

"Is there any chance in hell she'd show up here?"

"I doubt it. It's been six months now." Maddie shrugged, but realized she didn't really have a clue what Mary was capable of. "I have my address book, and I told her you and I had a falling out so she would hopefully think I'd gone somewhere else. I guess we can't completely rule it out though."

"I guess we'll cross that bridge if we come to it, right?"

"Hopefully, we never will."

"Hey, maybe you can move on with Savannah Wells." Dana winked and Maddie couldn't help but laugh at her expectant expression.

"I should go." Maddie got to her feet and started for the door, fully expecting Dana to follow her, but was surprised to find it wasn't the case. She smiled to herself as she walked out the door and headed for her car. It might be rather nice to move on with the sexy neighbor at that.

Chapter Four

W hat do you mean you're leaving?" Kelly asked after they'd been in the bar for barely more than an hour.

"I'm not feeling well," Savannah said, shaking her head and grimacing as though she had a stomachache. She wasn't in physical pain but mentally she just wasn't feeling it tonight. There was a certain new neighbor she couldn't get out of her head. Of course, she hadn't mentioned Maddie's visit to Kelly, because, why would she? "I think I must have undercooked the chicken or something."

"I feel fine," Kelly said, looking at her like she wasn't buying what Savannah was trying to sell. "You just need another beer."

"No," Savannah said, grabbing her arm before she could wave the bartender over. "I just want to go home and lie down, all right? We can do this some other time."

"I should have known you were planning to bail on me when you insisted on riding your motorcycle." Kelly turned her back to the bar and looked out at the dance floor. She leaned closer so Savannah could hear her, but she never looked at her. "Whatever. It doesn't matter. Not like we'd end up leaving together anyway, right?"

"Kel," Savannah said, feeling bad about lying to her, but not bad enough to come clean. "I really don't feel good. I didn't plan this."

"Just go," Kelly said, waving a dismissive hand in her direction. "But next time, I'm not paying for a single drink."

"Like you ever do," Savannah said with a chuckle.

"Yeah, it's a curse to look this good." Kelly grinned, and Savannah knew she wasn't really mad.

"You're an ass," Savannah said before hugging her. "You're my best friend, and I love you. Don't do anything I wouldn't do."

"Be careful on that bike," Kelly said when Savannah walked past her on her way to the door. "I expect it to be my inheritance, and I don't want it damaged."

Savannah just waved over her shoulder in response. Kelly was right about one thing. They usually went to the bars together, but rarely left together. It was a common occurrence for them to go home with women they picked up, and it was the reason they even went to these places at all. Like Lisa had said that morning—*you aren't going to meet a woman to marry in those clubs you go to.*

It took almost an hour for her to get home, and the first thing she noticed upon turning onto her cul-de-sac was the lights were on at Maddie's house. She put her bike into the garage and stood there looking next door, fighting the urge to go knock on the door. What would she say?

Just wanted to say good night.

I had to see you because you seem to have hijacked my brain.

Hi. I really need to taste your lips.

"Fuck," she said, turning away from the street and pushing the button to close the garage door. Like any of those lines would work. All she really wanted was to shove Maddie against the wall and have her way with her. No, more precisely, she wanted Maddie to shove *her* against the wall. Her step faltered as she entered the house. Where the hell had that thought come from? Savannah never let anyone, ever, take control of her. She shook her head and reached down to pick up Leo with one hand. "What's wrong with me, little man?"

He meowed and stared at her, his eyes half closed. She kissed his nose and set him back down on the floor with a sigh. After grabbing a beer and heading for the couch to try to relax and maybe watch a movie, she froze when there was a knock on the door. She glanced at Leo, who was running to the door to greet his company. As far as he was concerned, no one ever came over to see her. If they were there, it was all about him.

"Hold your horses," she said, assuming it would be Kelly. She was caught off guard when she saw Maddie standing there, the jersey Savannah had loaned her earlier folded neatly in her hands. "Uh, hi."

"I heard you come home, so I was hoping it was okay to come over." She looked over Savannah's shoulder into the living room, probably trying to see if she was alone.

"Yeah, of course." Savannah stepped aside and motioned her in. She took the jersey Maddie held out to her as she passed. "You didn't have to bring it back tonight."

"I was informed it was an authentic game worn jersey, so I was under the impression that made it pretty special. I wouldn't want to risk anything bad happening to it." Maddie smiled and winked at her, and Savannah had to turn away or risk doing something that had the potential to be rather embarrassing.

"Well, we play at least seventy games a year, so I have plenty of opportunities to get game worn jerseys." Savannah tossed it onto the chair she walked by on her way to the kitchen. "Would you like a beer? Or I have soda. Water, wine."

"A beer is fine."

Savannah was trying really hard to not freak out. There was a beautiful woman in her living room, and she was nervous. That like, literally, *never* happened. She closed her eyes and took a couple of calming breaths before popping the top off the bottle of beer and returned to find Maddie studying the pictures on her mantel.

"Those are my moms," Savannah said as she stood next to her and held the bottle out. "Lisa and Faith."

"You have two moms?" Maddie smiled as she glanced at her, and Savannah simply nodded in response. She took a drink and returned her attention to the photo. "That is so freaking cool."

"Maybe to a lesbian who didn't grow up with two moms."

"You just assume I'm a lesbian?" Maddie turned fully to face her and Savannah grimaced at having done exactly that.

"Deductive reasoning." Savannah gave her a shrug and met her eyes.

"Do tell."

"Well, earlier there was the comment about not usually using a woman's shower without at least knowing her name," Savannah said, then paused when Maddie smiled and gave her an almost imperceptible nod. "And I don't really think there are a lot of straight women who would say it was cool to have two moms. I apologize if I was wrong in my assumption."

"You weren't," Maddie said as she turned and moved to take a seat on the couch. Leo wasted no time getting on her lap. Savannah settled in on the other end, a safe distance away from Maddie. "So tell me why it wasn't cool for you to have two moms."

"Where do I begin?" Savannah looked at the ceiling and sighed. "Honestly, it was kind of cool, until I realized they didn't want me to turn out to be lesbian." She looked at Maddie, who appeared to be perplexed by the statement. Savannah gave her a wry smile. "They knew how hard it was for them, and they really wanted a better, or easier, life for me. Alas, it wasn't meant to be."

"So, did you have to come out to them?"

"Yeah. And it didn't go well. Lisa, the blonde in the pictures, spent the first six months after I told them trying to set me up with guys." Savannah couldn't help but laugh when Maddie did. It was such an infectious sound. "Once she realized I really was a lesbian, she decided to switch gears and set me up with women. Faith has given her a hard time about it for years, but she still tries to do it."

"You call them by their first names?"

"Yeah. Weird, right?"

"No," Maddie said, shaking her head and scratching Leo under the chin. Savannah was jealous of her cat. There was no way around it. "It kind of makes sense, actually. I'm sure it might have been confusing otherwise."

"Which is why they insisted on it the year I started first grade." Savannah took a drink of her beer before setting the bottle on the coffee table. "Who in your life is a big enough hockey fan to know the jersey was game worn? There aren't any rips or blood on it."

"Blood?" Maddie looked horrified. "Why would there be blood? I thought women didn't play physical. At least they don't in the Olympics."

"No, they don't," Savannah said. "But we do. And even if we didn't, there's always a chance of a high stick hitting you somewhere you aren't protected."

"Sounds brutal." Maddie shook her head and looked at the cat for a moment. "To answer your question though, it's my fourteen-year-old niece who noticed the black marks from the pucks on the jersey. It seems she has a bit of a crush on you. My brother-in-law's words, not mine."

"No offense, but she's about fifteen years too young for me. At least."

"That's reassuring."

"So," Savannah said, glancing away when Maddie looked at her because she was dangerously close to making a move on her off limits neighbor. No way could she look into those intense green eyes for any length of time and *not* make a move. "Are you living alone next door?"

"Is this your way of asking if I'm single?" Maddie winked at her when Savannah's head whipped around, and Savannah felt her cheeks begin to burn. "Because I am. Single. And living alone. How about you?"

"Perpetually single, yes," Savannah said with a nod.

"Why is that? Have you been hurt by someone you loved?"

"Nope, I've never been in a relationship. I refuse to allow anyone to have so much power over me and my happiness." It was a lie, but Savannah saw no reason to tell her about college. About how Shauna had not only crushed her heart, but shattered it completely.

"Why do you feel that way?"

"I don't know anyone whose parents aren't divorced. I don't believe in love as a long-lasting entity."

"How long have your moms been together?"

"Since before I was born, but it doesn't mean they haven't had their share of problems."

"Everyone has problems, Savannah, but that doesn't mean they don't love each other. And not every marriage ends in divorce. My parents have been married for almost forty years."

Savannah didn't want to be having this conversation, especially with someone she'd only just met earlier that day. Yes, she wanted to get to know Maddie better, but she wasn't used to tackling such heavy subjects with anyone other than Kelly.

"Why are you single?" Savannah asked in an obvious attempt to change the subject.

"Subtlety isn't your strong point, is it?" Maddie laughed and Savannah chuckled as she shook her head. "Okay, so your private life is off limits, but not mine. Got it. I moved here a few months ago after my girlfriend decided she'd be happier with someone else. In fact, she'd been happier with someone else for about three months before she finally let me know."

"She must be insane," Savannah said before she could stop herself.

"Why do you say that?" Maddie had been watching Leo as she scratched under his chin but raised her gaze to meet Savannah's eyes.

Savannah tried to look away. Really, she did. But Maddie had some sort of force field surrounding her and she found it physically impossible to do anything but stare into her eyes. Yeah. A force field. It was the only logical explanation, right? She struggled to come up with something witty to say in response to Maddie's question, but nothing was coming to mind.

"Have you looked at yourself?" she finally managed to say. "If you were my girlfriend, I wouldn't need to look anywhere else for happiness."

"Thank you, but considering you're *perpetually* single, I'm not sure your opinion would hold much sway."

"You're probably right," Savannah said with a shrug. "But it's still my opinion."

"You're sweet." Maddie nudged Leo to get him off her lap before getting to her feet. "And I think I should go before I do something I'll no doubt regret."

Savannah walked her to the door where they stood in awkward silence for a moment. Savannah sighed and placed her hand on Maddie's arm, a move she regretted almost instantly because of the spark seeming to ignite between the two of them. In spite of the regret, she left her hand where it was.

"Anytime you need to use my shower, it's yours," she said with a grin.

"Good to know," Maddie replied with a nod. She reached behind her and opened the door before leaning in and kissing Savannah's cheek. Her lips lingered a moment, but then she pulled away when Savannah's hand moved up her arm to her shoulder. "Good night, Savannah."

"Good night," she replied, an overwhelming feeling of disappointment washing over her as she watched Maddie walk out her door. She locked up for the night and went into her bedroom. Leo jumped up on the bed and looked at her, an undeniable question in his eyes. "I don't know, little man. I can see myself getting in over my head with this one."

CHAPTER FIVE

H oly hell, there's a lot of people here this year," Kelly said as she took a seat at the table next to Savannah.

"I think every year there's more than the year before," Savannah replied, scanning the crowd for her parents and brother. The yearly Fourth of July carnival had really taken off since the team started doing it six years before. It was a fundraiser for multiple charities in the area, and people always seemed to open their wallets more freely when it was for a good cause.

"Let's get this party started," Alex White, center to Savannah's and Kelly's wing positions said from Kelly's other side. Alex had been new to the team the previous season, and it hadn't taken their line any time at all to click. It was almost as if they'd been playing together for years.

"She's cute, isn't she?" Kelly said for the hundredth time, leaning close to Savannah so no one else could hear. Savannah chuckled.

"Do you ever stop?" she asked.

"Nope," Kelly said as she sat back to wait for the line of autograph seekers to be opened for them. "And I probably never will."

"Maybe you should tell her you have a crush on her."

"Please," Kelly said with a look of horror. "Kelly Rawlins does not have crushes."

"No, she just lusts after women," Savannah said.

"Damn right," Kelly said before turning to talk to Alex.

Savannah, still scanning the crowd for her parents, sucked in a breath when her eyes landed on Maddie Scott a few yards away talking with a man and woman. She looked down at her hands resting on the table in front of her and tried to still her racing heart. *What the fuck?* She hadn't spoken with Maddie since the night she'd moved in next door, and she had no idea why her body was reacting in such a visceral way now.

"Are you all right?" Kelly asked quietly. "You look really pale."

"Fine." Savannah nodded and looked at her with a smile. "Just getting my game face on."

Kelly didn't look convinced, but Savannah couldn't worry about her right now. She needed to figure out her own uncharacteristic reaction to seeing a beautiful woman. The first few minutes of signing autographs went smoothly, but then Kelly suddenly nudged her with an elbow and jutted her chin to Savannah's left.

"Isn't that your neighbor?" Kelly asked while still signing and engaging with the kids seeking her signature.

Savannah glanced to where Kelly indicated and saw Maddie with a camera, taking their picture. A young girl was pointing at Savannah and pulling on Maddie's sleeve as she did so. Maddie nodded and smiled at Savannah.

"Yeah," she answered as she tore her eyes away from Maddie. She smiled at the next girl in line who was waiting for her signature on one of the promotional eight-by-tens the team was handing out to everyone who was entering the event. She asked for the girl's name before personalizing a message to her.

"Thank you," the girl said, her eyes wide. She couldn't have been more than seven, and Savannah smiled at the way she jumped up and down before moving on to Kelly.

"What's her name?" Kelly asked, blatantly staring at Maddie. "Your neighbor."

"Madison Scott." Savannah looked up and saw Maddie standing in front of her with the girl who'd been pulling on her sleeve. "Hi."

"Hi, this is Amy, my niece," Maddie said, her arm around the girl's shoulders. "She wants me to take her picture with you if that's all right."

Savannah looked around for a moment, knowing they weren't supposed to take pictures with the fans while they were signing. It slowed down the line, and if she allowed it for one, they'd have to allow it for all of them. They could very well be there all night then.

"Can we do it later?" Savannah asked. "I'll be done here in about an hour."

"We aren't supposed to stop and pose for pictures," Kelly explained with a smile Savannah thought was a little too flirty. "We'll be over by the games when we're done here."

"Oh, okay." Maddie smiled at Savannah again, and Savannah was happy she seemed totally oblivious to Kelly's flirting. Maddie leaned down to talk to her niece. "I'll be over there with your parents, okay?"

"Yeah," Amy said with a nod. When Maddie was gone, she slid Savannah's photo in front of her. "You're my favorite player."

"Well, thank you," Savannah said as she signed it to Amy. "Do you go to many of the games?"

"My dad takes me to most of them. We always sit right behind the bench."

"I'll make sure you get a puck or stick the next time I see you there." Savannah smiled at her as Amy took a couple of small steps toward Kelly.

"That would be awesome, thanks!"

"Suck up," Kelly muttered under her breath.

"Jealous much?" Savannah laughed at her.

The rest of their time at the table went smoothly, so when Jen Hilton and her wingers arrived for their turn, Savannah got up without a word and walked away. There was no love lost between her and Hilton, and the less she had to interact with her, the better.

She made her way toward the area where the carnival games were set up, but she stopped in her tracks when she saw their coach, Gail, standing with Maddie and looking at the pictures she'd been taking. *What the heck is that about?*

"Wells, come here for a minute," Gail said when she looked her way and saw her watching them.

"What's up?" Savannah asked as she joined them. Maddie smiled at her, and Savannah tried to ignore the way her stomach fluttered at the attention. She smiled back at her and turned her attention to Gail.

"I'm sure you've met your new neighbor by now," Gail said, motioning to Maddie.

"I have, but a heads-up would have been nice since you sold her the house."

"Really?" Gail looked between them, and Savannah would swear Gail knew everything she was thinking about Maddie. "Interesting. Anyway, she's also been hired by the owners to be the official photographer of the Warriors this year. She'll be at the games taking action shots, and she'll also be taking promotional stills for the game-day programs and for this event next summer."

"Okay," Savannah glanced at Maddie, wondering why she hadn't mentioned any of this to her. "Welcome aboard."

"Thank you," Maddie said with a nod. "I'm photographing a wedding later this month, but after that, since you're the captain of the team, I'll need to coordinate with you to schedule everyone for the promo shots."

"Sure, just let me know when." Savannah looked at Gail, hoping she'd see the question she was asking with her eyes. Maddie wasn't referring to Court and Lana's wedding, was she? That would just be too weird.

"Lana knows Maddie from her gig as photographer for the orchestra in Chicago, and she and Court have hired her to shoot their wedding," Gail said, reading her perfectly. "And I think this would be a good time to go find my hubby and kids. Excuse me."

Savannah watched Gail walk away, and even though she wanted to do so herself, she couldn't. What was it about Madison Scott that made Savannah want to get to know her better? She mentally shook herself before meeting Maddie's eyes.

"So you know Court and Lana?"

"I do," Maddie answered.

"That would have been nice to know too," Savannah said under her breath just as Kelly walked up to join them.

"Are you going to introduce me?" she asked as she slung an arm around Savannah's shoulders.

"No," Savannah said reflexively, but then cringed slightly at her own insolence.

"Well, that isn't rude, is it?" Kelly laughed and held her hand out to Maddie. "I'm Kelly Rawlins. Savannah's best friend."

"Madison Scott," she replied, accepting the offered hand. "Savannah's next-door neighbor."

"I know," Kelly said. "We watched you move in."

"Oh?" Maddie looked at Savannah, an eyebrow raised in question.

"No, you watched her moving in," Savannah said with a shake of her head. "I was minding my own business."

"Whatever," Kelly said with a dismissive wave. "Hey, when this is done, we're going back to Savannah's moms' house for a barbeque and to watch the fireworks. You should join us."

"Faith and Lisa, right?" Maddie asked Savannah.

"Oh, you know them?" Kelly seemed surprised, and Savannah wanted to blend into the crowd to get away from them. She hadn't told Kelly about spending any time with Maddie.

"No, Savannah told me about them."

"No shit?" Kelly looked at Savannah, who just shrugged. "I didn't know you two knew each other so well."

"Aunt Maddie," said Amy as she ran up to them. Savannah could have kissed her for saving her from this particular conversation right now. Amy looked at Savannah and smiled shyly. "Can we take the picture now?"

"Sure," Savannah said quickly before glancing at Kelly. "I'll catch up with you in a minute."

Kelly didn't look happy, but she finally nodded once and turned to walk away. When Savannah refocused her attention to Maddie, she was met with a questioning look, which she chose to ignore.

"Where should we stand?" Amy asked, oblivious to the uneasiness Savannah was feeling.

"How about right where you are?" Maddie asked before raising the camera to focus on them. Amy stood next to Savannah and she put an arm around Amy's shoulders to pose for the picture. Once it was done, Amy ran off, probably to find her parents. "You look much better in your jersey than I did."

"I doubt that very much," Savannah said, remembering the moment she saw Maddie walking out of her bathroom wearing the very same jersey. "You're welcome to come by, for the barbecue and fireworks."

"I kind of got the impression you didn't want me there."

"Not true." Savannah stood with her hands in the back pockets of her shorts and looked around at the people walking by. "There's a great view of the fireworks from the backyard, and a lot less people than if you went down to the river. Unless you have plans, that is."

"I do have plans, with my sister and her family."

"They're welcome too. Lisa always makes way more food than we need, and she always says the more the merrier."

"Will the whole team be there?" Maddie asked, not sure she wanted to intrude on family time at the Wells household. It just seemed like it might be safer if there were other people around. She'd stayed away from Savannah since that first day because she didn't trust herself to not touch her. She wasn't sure she'd ever felt this level of attraction to anyone before.

"No, just Kelly. Alex might stop by, and maybe Charlotte, our goaltender, but that would be it besides my moms, my brother and his family, and Court's sister with her two kids." Savannah shrugged. "I'd love for you to come."

Maddie looked away to hide the grin caused by the double entendre, and saw her sister waving, trying to get her attention. She waved back before looking at Savannah, who had obviously realized what she'd said based on the level of color in her cheeks. Maddie pulled out her cell phone and swiped the screen before opening her text messaging app.

"Give me your number," she said, readying her thumbs to enter it. When Savannah was done reciting the number to her, she typed in a quick message and hit send.

I'd love to come.

She smiled and winked when Savannah's cheeks turned an even deeper shade of red as their eyes met. Maddie returned the phone to her pocket and sighed.

"I'm being summoned, and I'm sure Kelly's waiting for you," she said. "Text me the address, and if we can't make it, I'll let you know."

CHAPTER SIX

M addie tried to stay occupied with her sister's family, but every time she saw a woman wearing a Warriors jersey, her attention wandered. The whole team was wearing their home white jerseys, and who the hell could have guessed so many of them had black hair? If not for the names on the jerseys, she would have thought half of them were Savannah from the back.

"I can't believe we're going to spend the Fourth of July with Savannah Wells." Amy was so excited, it had to have been the twentieth time she'd said the same thing. Maddie was just happy they were almost there so she'd stop saying it.

"And her family," Dana pointed out from the front seat. Maddie had chosen to carpool with them because it seemed silly to take her own car since they'd picked her up that morning and she'd already spent the whole day with them.

"She really has two moms?" Amy asked again. Maddie rolled her eyes, causing Dana to stifle a laugh.

"Yes, she really does," Maddie said.

"That is so awesome." Amy turned her head to look out the window, a sure sign she was going to be quiet for at least a few minutes.

"Here we are," Trent said as he pulled in behind a car parked in the street in front of the house. He shut the car off and turned to look at Amy. "You behave yourself, and mind your manners, you understand?"

"Yes," Amy answered with an eye roll of her own. "I'm not five."

Dana laughed, which earned her a stern glare from Trent. Maddie smiled when Dana tried her best to look serious.

"You aren't too old for me to bend you over my knee," Trent said.

"Promise?" Dana asked him with a wink.

"So gross," Amy said before opening her door and getting out.

Maddie laughed then, and Trent turned his glare on her. "Do I need to have a talking to with you too? Tell you to mind your manners?"

"No, sir, you don't," Maddie assured him. "And if you try bending *me* over your knee, you'll end up in a choke hold."

He raised his hands in surrender before they all got out and made their way up the front walk. The door opened just as Maddie was about to knock, and her heart rate quickened at the sight of Savannah wearing shorts and a rather tight fitting tank top.

"I'm so happy you all could make it," Savannah said.

"Thank you for inviting us," Trent said as he shook her hand.

"Mind your manners," Dana said close to Maddie's ear. "You look like you're about to start drooling."

Maddie felt her cheeks grow hot as she quickly brought her gaze up to Savannah's face and she realized she'd been caught staring at her breasts. *Real smooth. Could you be any more obvious?*

"Come in," Savannah said as she stepped back and motioned them through the door. She winked when Maddie walked past her, and Maddie wanted to turn around and run away. "You can just walk through the house to the patio door. Everyone is outside."

They walked slowly, waiting for Savannah to get to the patio doors first, because it just seemed weird to walk out there without knowing anyone else. Savannah seemed to sense this and led them all out to the patio where there were two older women tending the grill side by side. She put her arm around one of them and turned her around.

"This is my mom Lisa and my other mom Faith," she said as they both smiled and wiped their hands on their aprons before shaking hands with their guests. "Lisa, Faith, this is my next-door neighbor Madison Scott; her sister, Dana; and her husband, Trent; and their daughter, Amy. Did I get all the names right?"

"Perfect," Trent said with a big grin as he shook their hands. "It's a pleasure to meet you lovely ladies."

"And you as well," Faith said.

Lisa was smiling and watching Maddie with what seemed to be a little too much interest for Maddie's liking, and it made her a little uncomfortable. She shifted her weight from one foot to the other and glanced at Savannah, who seemed to understand her uneasiness.

"Next-door neighbor?" Lisa asked as she took Maddie by the arm and tried to lead her away. Savannah stopped her with a hand on Lisa's shoulder and a firm shake of her head.

"I can see those wheels spinning, Lisa, and you need to stop," Savannah said.

"Stop what?" Lisa asked, feigning innocence so obvious Maddie almost laughed out loud. She had a feeling Lisa was going to try her matchmaking abilities on the two of them.

"Lisa," Faith said in a tone that obviously got through to her because Lisa sighed and let go of Maddie's arm.

"We'll talk later," Lisa said to Maddie before returning to her grilling duties.

"Help yourself to whatever you want to drink. Everything is in the coolers," Faith told them.

"Beer?" Savannah asked, and Maddie nodded. She gave Dana, Trent, and Amy their drinks before grabbing a couple of beers for them. She leaned in closer and spoke into Maddie's ear. "Come with me."

Maddie followed her out to the yard where there were lawn chairs and umbrellas set up to give some shade to the guests. Since there wasn't anyone else there yet, Maddie assumed the real party wouldn't start until closer to the scheduled fireworks.

"This is a nice house," Madison said as she looked at the two-story structure in front of them. The back patio was huge, large enough for three picnic tables end to end, and was covered by a second story deck the length of the house. "Is this where you grew up?"

"Yes," Savannah said, looking up at the second story. "This is the only house Lisa and Faith have lived in since before I was born. My brother and his family stay here when they come to town for holidays."

"It's nice they have a place to stay." Madison took in the rest of the yard, including the swimming pool which was surrounded by a fence a few feet away from them. "So what was all that with Lisa?"

"Remember I told you she likes to set me up on blind dates?" Savannah looked at her with a sheepish grin, and Maddie nodded, happy she'd read the situation correctly. "She was going into matchmaker mode when she found out you were my next-door neighbor. She can be irritating at times, but she's totally harmless, trust me."

"I think it's sweet," Maddie said. Savannah let out a dramatic gasp and placed a hand on her own chest, causing Maddie to laugh. "Really, it's sweet. She wants you to be happy. What's wrong with that?"

"I am happy. At least happier than I would be going out on Lisa's ill-advised blind dates."

"Ill-advised?" Maddie smiled, knowing this would be a story she definitely wanted to hear.

"I'll tell you about it sometime," Savannah said. "Suffice it to say the world is lucky Lisa Wells didn't decide to become a professional matchmaker."

"Is this a private party, or can anyone join?"

Maddie glanced up and saw Kelly standing next to her. Kelly smiled and winked at her, which gave Maddie the distinct impression she was a player. No doubt the kind who had a different woman in every city her team played in. Maybe more than one.

Probably a different one each time they stopped in any city. Maddie looked at Savannah for a moment and wondered if she was the same way.

"It's nice to see you again, Madison Scott," Kelly said, pulling up a chair without waiting for an answer to her question.

"You too." Maddie nodded. Maybe she could have a little fun at Kelly's expense. "It's Carrie, right?"

Savannah snickered as she looked away, and Maddie almost felt guilty for teasing Kelly when she appeared honestly hurt she didn't remember her name.

"Kelly," she said before kicking Savannah in the leg.

"Ouch," Savannah said as she rubbed her leg and glared at Kelly.

"Serves you right," Kelly said.

"Not many women forget her name," Savannah explained to Maddie. "So she's a little sensitive when one does."

"Piss off," Kelly told Savannah. When Savannah didn't move, Kelly looked at her. "Seriously, Van, piss off. Go get me a beer or something."

Maddie wanted to offer to go get it herself, because she had a feeling she knew what was coming. As attractive as Kelly was, she wasn't interested. It was Savannah who got her juices flowing, and she really didn't want her to leave her alone with Kelly. She sighed and forced a smile when Savannah got to her feet.

"You call her Van?" Maddie asked as she watched Savannah walk back toward the house. She realized she was staring when Kelly didn't answer and she turned her head to find Kelly watching her watching Savannah. She didn't look amused, but rather she seemed irritated.

"Yeah, we've known each other forever," Kelly finally said when Maddie focused her attention squarely on her. "We grew up together. Hell, we even went to college together. And now we play on the same team together."

"That must be nice." Maddie took a drink of her beer and forced herself to keep her eyes on Kelly. "I've never had a best friend like that. Everyone scattered after high school and lost touch. Not that I would want to see any of them again."

"That's too bad," Kelly said. "I don't know what I would have done without Van in our younger years. Maybe after you've known her for twenty-five years you can call her Van too. Of course you and I will be old and gray, and no doubt playing with our grandchildren by then."

"Pretty sure of yourself, aren't you?" Maddie asked, barely stopping herself from spewing her beer all over Kelly. She wiped her mouth and shook her head.

"Just confident." Kelly lifted one shoulder and relaxed in her chair with a smug smile. "With good reason, I might add."

"I'm sure." Maddie glanced over Kelly's shoulder and saw Savannah approaching with a finger across her lips to indicate she shouldn't let on what was about to happen. She noticed a chunk of ice in Savannah's hand and refocused on Kelly while somehow managing not to smile. "You certainly exude confidence."

"Have dinner with me some time." Kelly finished speaking and leaned forward just as Savannah reached her and dropped the ice down the back of the jersey she was still wearing from the carnival earlier. She shot out of the chair and started dancing around to get rid of it. Maddie was laughing not only because of the funky dance Kelly was doing, but because Savannah was literally rolling on the ground laughing at her. "You're a fucking asshole, Wells!"

After finally getting the ice to fall out the back of her jersey, Kelly began walking toward Savannah with a menacing look that scared Maddie. She wouldn't really hurt her best friend, would she? She got to her feet with the intention of helping Savannah, but a stern voice from the porch stopped Kelly in her tracks.

"Kelly Rawlins!" Faith yelled loudly. "There are children present! Come here right now!"

Maddie wouldn't have thought anyone could intimidate Kelly, but she looked like a frightened child as she glared one more time at Savannah before making her way to the porch.

"That was awesome," Savannah said as she finally made her way back to her seat.

"It was pretty funny," Maddie said. She watched as Faith was obviously doing a decent job of chastising Kelly if the slump of her shoulders was any indication. "What's up with that?"

"Faith can swear like a sailor with the best of them, but not when there are kids around," Savannah said. "It's a thing with her, and Kelly is well aware of it. If I'd said what she did, I'd be the one up there getting an earful, trust me."

CHAPTER SEVEN

"Y ou really are an ass, Wells," Kelly said to her a couple of hours later. It was the first time she'd spoken to her since getting in trouble with Faith, and it was also the first time Savannah found herself alone, as Maddie had gone inside to use the bathroom.

"You're right, I am," Savannah said with a nod. She couldn't help but chuckle as she remembered the dance Kelly did though. "What the hell was that, some kind of tribal dance?"

"It was my own special 'holy hell that's fucking cold' dance." Kelly laughed too, but she shook her head. "Why did you do it?"

"It started out as a joke, but as I got closer I'd actually decided not to do it."

"But you did. Why?"

"Because you were hitting on my neighbor," Savannah said. She looked at Kelly but was confused by what she was feeling. Honestly, she shouldn't be feeling anything for Maddie, but it didn't change the fact she was. Maybe it was just lust and she should sleep with her to get it out of her system. No, Maddie wasn't the type for a one-night stand. She wasn't sure how she knew it, but she did. "No sleeping with a neighbor, remember?"

"I'm telling you, that was not a part of the original rules." Kelly shook her head as Savannah's brother, Noah, joined them.

"Rules for what?" he asked, looking back and forth between the two of them.

"Dating," Kelly answered before finishing her beer.

Noah looked at Savannah, one eyebrow raised in question. She knew he was well aware of the fact neither of them *dated* anyone. Savannah shook her head at him, hoping he'd get the message she didn't want to talk about it. At least not now, but she would no doubt explain it to him later when Kelly wasn't around. Savannah told Noah pretty much everything, and he did the same.

"I am so glad I'm not dating anymore," he said. "I don't do well with rules."

"Neither do I," Kelly said. She got up and walked away without another word.

"So, your new neighbor," Noah said when they were alone. He wiggled his eyebrows, causing her to laugh. "Hot damn."

"Does your wife know you objectify other women?"

"Of course she does. As long as I don't objectify her, she's perfectly fine with it." He laced his fingers together and put them behind his head as he watched her. "Please tell me you're hitting that, sis."

"You are such a dog," she said, kicking him softly in the leg.

"Then you're not." He actually seemed to be disappointed and Savannah just shook her head. "You should, you know. How convenient for you having her right next door."

"It's because she's right next door I won't," Savannah told him. She sighed. "If she lived somewhere else, I would have already."

"So you admit she's hot."

"I have a pulse, don't I?" She took a drink of her beer to cover the fact she might be blushing at the thoughts running through her mind. There was no doubt Maddie Scott was hot. And Savannah was increasingly worried she might end up breaking her own rules.

When Maddie opened the bathroom door, she was surprised to find Kelly standing on the other side, a grin on her face. She had the distinct feeling it was no accident Kelly was waiting there for her.

"Excuse me," she said, trying to slip past her. She was relieved when Kelly let her go, but after a couple of steps, she felt a hand on her arm.

"Madison, wait," she said. "Can we talk for a minute? You never gave me an answer when I asked you out to dinner."

"I don't think it's a good idea." Maddie shook her head and took a small step back. She didn't want to give Kelly the impression she was interested in her.

"Why not? It's just dinner, not a marriage proposal," Kelly said with a chuckle.

"Look, I'm flattered, but I just broke up with my girlfriend, and I'm really not interested in dating right now." Maddie figured there was no reason to tell her it had been a few months since the breakup, and she was definitely over her ex. Actually, she was over her not long after finding out she'd been cheating. "You understand, right?"

"Sure," Kelly said with a nod, but Maddie could tell she wasn't used to being turned down. "Let me know if you ever change your mind. I could show you a really good time."

Kelly winked at her, and Maddie really didn't know what to say. So instead of saying anything, she turned and headed toward the patio door. As soon as she stepped outside, she found herself being sucked into a conversation with Lisa and Faith. Or maybe an argument was a more apt descriptor.

"Lisa, you need to stop," Faith was saying, but Lisa just waved a hand in her wife's direction and turned her attention to Maddie. "Oh, for crying out loud."

"Madison, dear, can I speak with you for a moment?" Lisa asked as she took her by the elbow and led her to the end of the picnic tables, away from everyone else who was there. Once they were settled, Lisa smiled at her and reached across the table to pat her hand. "Tell me, Madison, are you dating anyone?"

"Not at the moment, no," she answered. She had a suspicion she knew what was coming, but she decided to listen to what Lisa had to say. Maddie glanced out to the yard where Savannah and Noah seemed to be in deep conversation.

"Are you interested in men, women, or both?"

"Women," Maddie answered with a chuckle. "Definitely women."

"I just needed to make sure, so I had to ask," Lisa said.

"What is this about?" Maddie decided to play dumb and not let Lisa know Savannah had already warned her about Lisa's matchmaking ambitions.

"Savannah." Lisa leaned across the table and spoke in a conspiratorial tone. "She needs someone to take care of her, but she'll never admit it. If you would ask her on a date, I'll be in your debt."

"Can she not find her own dates?" Maddie managed to ask with a straight face. "Is there something wrong with her?"

"What? No, of course not," Lisa said, looking appalled at the mere suggestion. "She spends too much time with Kelly at a bar in Allentown, and I know she's never going to find a good woman in a place like that."

"I'll think about it, okay?" Maddie said. "I'm not sure it would be a good idea to date my next-door neighbor. What if it didn't work out? That could be really awkward."

"What's going on?" Savannah asked as she joined them. She looked at Lisa with a disapproving glare.

"Nothing, sweetie," Lisa said, appearing as innocent as could be. Maddie struggled not to laugh out loud. "We were just talking."

"Sure you were," Savannah said sarcastically. She turned her attention to Maddie then. "The fireworks are about to start. Join me?"

Maddie nodded and they both stood to head back out to the yard. Maddie stopped at the coolers before they stepped off the deck.

"Another beer?" she asked.

"I'm switching to water," Savannah said with a shake of her head. "I drove here on my motorcycle and don't want to keep drinking."

Maddie nodded and grabbed a couple of bottles of water for them. She was pretty sure Savannah had only had a couple of beers in the past four hours and was impressed she didn't want to drive while impaired. As she was following Savannah out to their seats, Maddie was struck with what she thought was a brilliant idea.

"What was she really talking to you about?" Savannah asked when they were settled.

"She wants me to ask you out." Maddie set her bottle on the ground next to her chair and glanced at Savannah, who appeared to be getting angry.

"I'm going to kill her."

"Just relax," Maddie said, reaching out and placing her hand on Savannah's forearm. "I have an idea. We can talk about it later."

CHAPTER EIGHT

S avannah offered to give Maddie a ride home since she'd come to the house with her sister. It had seemed logical when she suggested it, but riding the ten miles home with Maddie behind her on the bike was some kind of sweet torture. She'd found it hard to breathe with Maddie's arms around her waist, and her breasts pressed against her back.

She sat on the bike for a few moments after shutting the engine off, but Maddie made no move to dismount. Savannah closed her eyes and took a deep breath before placing her hand over both of Maddie's, still resting on her stomach.

"You need to get off first," Savannah said, cringing at her words. It seemed she was destined to speak in double entendres while she was around Maddie. A shiver ran through her at Maddie's throaty chuckle close to her ear.

"If you insist," Maddie said as she let go of her.

Once they were both standing next to the bike, Savannah placed her helmet on a shelf in the garage along with the one she'd borrowed from Lisa for Maddie to wear, and then stood there awkwardly, wondering if she should invite Maddie inside. She wanted to, but there was a part of her that thought it would be a bad idea.

"Do you want to come in?" she finally asked when it became apparent Maddie wasn't going to leave on her own. "You made a cryptic comment about some idea in regards to Lisa's matchmaking. Maybe you should tell me about it."

Maddie smiled and followed her inside where they were assaulted by Leo's demands for dinner. Maddie picked him up and cuddled him as she followed Savannah to the kitchen. Her cat was getting more action than she was. Lucky little bastard.

Once Leo was fed and finally happy, Savannah grabbed them both a beer and motioned for Maddie to follow her to the living room. They settled in on opposite ends of the couch and Savannah looked at her, eager to hear her idea as long as it involved Lisa stopping trying to set her up on dates she had no interest in. That thought gave her an idea. She wasn't sure Maddie would agree to it, but it was worth a shot.

"Listen, this might sound a little crazy, but would you be willing to pretend you and I are dating?" Savannah realized how off the wall it sounded when she actually said the words out loud. "I'm sorry, forget I suggested it. So what's your idea?"

"Well, to be honest, it's what you just proposed." Maddie seemed a little nervous, which Savannah thought was sexy as hell. She ran her fingers through her hair, and Savannah wondered what it would feel like to do it herself. Was Maddie's hair as soft as it looked? "I was going to say maybe we should pretend to be dating. I mean, if she thinks we're really seeing each other, then she'll back off, right? It's probably a horrible idea. You can tell me it's a horrible idea."

"It's not a great idea," Savannah said, rethinking the entire thing. But she quickly changed her mind when she saw the disappointment in Maddie's eyes. She never wanted to see anything there but happiness. She shook her head and moved closer to Maddie so she could take her hand. "But since I brought it up first it's not a horrible idea. It could actually work, but are you sure you'd want to do that for me?"

"A little full of yourself, aren't you?" They both laughed softly as Maddie looked down at their hands and squeezed Savannah's gently. "But to answer your question, yes, I would do that for you."

"What happens if you find a woman you really want to date?"

"I don't think that's going to happen," Maddie said quietly as she shook her head. Savannah's pulse took off when Maddie's gaze dropped to her lips before snapping back to her eyes. Maddie chewed on her bottom lip for a moment, and Savannah had to stifle a groan at the sight. "But if it does, then I guess we'd have to put a fake end to our fake relationship."

This could actually turn out to be a brilliant idea. Not only would Lisa back off, but she'd get to spend more time with this beautiful woman who seemed to have a knack for throwing her off kilter. And an added benefit was the fact Kelly would be forced to stop flirting with Maddie.

"We could give it a try, if you really want to," she finally said with a nod. "We'd probably have to spend a lot of time together."

"I don't think it would be too much of a hardship, do you?" Maddie winked and smiled, obviously no longer nervous.

"Not at all," Savannah answered as her stomach seemed to flutter. *What the hell?* It was probably time to end the evening, or she might end up doing something she'd no doubt regret. She pulled her hand away and moved back to her end of the couch. "Maybe we can get together in the next couple of days and hammer out some details."

"Sure," Maddie said. She seemed to pick up on Savannah's mood and got to her feet. "It's getting late, and I should probably be getting home."

Savannah followed her to the door but ran right into her when Maddie abruptly stopped and turned to face her. She instinctively placed her hands on Maddie's hips to keep her from falling, and found herself captured by Maddie's green eyes.

"I'd say I'm sorry, but it would be a lie," Maddie whispered. "I didn't know you'd be so close behind me."

"I'm sorry for tailgating," Savannah quipped, but it was a lie for her too. Anything that would land Maddie in her arms wasn't something to apologize for. Plus, following so close was the only way to keep her eyes from wandering down to Maddie's ass and legs.

"You know, it's a bit difficult to leave while you're holding me like this."

Then don't leave. It scared Savannah to realize how close those words were to coming out of her mouth. She started to pull her hands away, but Maddie stopped her by covering them with her own and holding them in place.

"I'm going to kiss you now," Maddie said. She must have seen the surprise Savannah felt because she gave her a lopsided smile and gave her an excuse. "You know, just for practice. I have a feeling Lisa won't believe we're seeing each other if we aren't convincing at being affectionate."

"We have to be convincing," Savannah said with a nod. She closed her eyes against the torrent of desire running through her. She leaned into the touch when Maddie cupped her cheek and slowly ran her thumb across her bottom lip. She opened her eyes again and saw the desire swirling in Maddie's.

Savannah felt out of breath, and if the rapid rise and fall of Maddie's chest was any indication, she was too. Unable to hold back any longer, Savannah gripped her hips tighter and pulled Maddie's body against her. Maddie snaked her arms around her neck and leaned closer, stopping only when their lips were a fraction of an inch apart.

"You are so amazingly sexy," she whispered, and then pressed their lips together softly.

Savannah thought her knees were going to give out. Her last coherent thought was that she'd never been kissed like this before. Or maybe she'd just never *let* herself be kissed like this before. She parted her lips to allow Maddie's tongue inside, and all thought ceased to exist. All she could concentrate on was the insistent throbbing between her legs. Oh, and the way Maddie's body felt against her own, and the incredible things her tongue was doing to her. She finally pulled away when she realized she needed to breathe. She rested her forehead against Maddie's and sighed.

"Holy crap," she said.

"I'll second that," Maddie said. "And can I just add, *wow.*"

"You can." Savannah chuckled. She took a step back, knowing if they stood this close together for much longer, she'd have no choice but to pick her up and carry her to the bedroom. "I'll call you tomorrow?"

"Yeah. Tomorrow."

Savannah stood on her porch watching until Maddie made it safely into her own house. She went back inside and leaned back against the door after she'd closed it. Leo came over after a moment and began playing with her feet. She picked him up and kissed his nose.

"I'm in so much trouble, my little man," she said as she turned off the lights and headed toward her bedroom. He began to purr and swiped his tongue across her chin a couple of times. "So much trouble."

CHAPTER NINE

"A re you busy today?" Savannah asked when she called Maddie a few days later. It was the weekend, and she had the urge to take a ride on her motorcycle. She hadn't even hesitated to call Maddie when she thought about her going along.

"Not at all," Maddie answered, sounding happy to hear from her. "What did you have in mind?"

"A ride, and maybe a short hike along a part of the Appalachian Trail," Savannah said as she was filling up a couple of water bottles.

"I'd love to. When do we leave?"

"As soon as you're ready just come on over."

It was only about twenty minutes before her doorbell rang, and her pulse began to race at the anticipation of seeing Maddie again. She opened the door and smiled at her as she motioned her in. Of course Leo was right there begging for attention from his new favorite person. Savannah had to admit while she was jealous of him, he did have impeccable taste in women. Maybe Lisa should have trained him to find her dates. He certainly couldn't have done any worse than her.

They stopped after walking the trail for about an hour and sat on a large rock just off the path. Maddie dug through her backpack they'd filled with their water bottles and some food. Savannah accepted the peanut butter and jelly sandwich she handed to her and took a big bite.

"So, how is this dating thing going to work?" Maddie asked after swallowing a bite of her own sandwich.

"Just like this," Savannah said with a grin, her arms spread out to encompass the great outdoors. "Or do you not like this as a date?"

"I think it's fantastic," Maddie said as she slapped a mosquito that landed on her leg.

"I guess I should have remembered to bring bug spray. Sorry about that."

"No, I'm serious," Maddie said, placing a hand on Savannah's thigh. "I'd much rather be doing this than sitting in a movie theater or some dark restaurant. This is perfect."

"We should probably tell each other about ourselves. To make it seem authentic, I mean."

"What would you like to know?" Maddie took a drink of water and looked at her.

"I don't know," Savannah said with a shrug. She wanted to know everything about Maddie if she was being honest, but how did she admit to that? "Favorite color, food, movies, music. You aren't a Republican, are you?"

"No," Maddie said with a chuckle. "Never have been, and never will be. Let's see, blue, pizza, all kinds of music, and I have a strange love for horror movies. They scare the crap out of me, but I love them."

"Horror movies, huh?" Savannah said, giving her a mock look of disgust.

"Is that a bad thing?"

"No, I just never understood the appeal. They all just seem so far-fetched, you know?" Savannah found herself wondering if they watched a horror movie together, would Maddie allow her to hold and protect her? She gave herself a mental shake. "Give me a good psychological thriller any day."

"I like those too," Maddie said with a nod. "Are you going to tell me your favorites?"

"Green, steak, and my phone has a little bit of every kind of music on it." Savannah finished her sandwich and leaned back, her hands on the rock behind her. "And don't laugh, but I love *The Sound of Music.*"

Right on cue, Maddie burst out laughing. Savannah stared at her. She wasn't even trying to hide her reaction. Savannah leaned forward and frowned at her. She didn't laugh at the horror films Maddie loves, even though she'd wanted to.

"I told you not to laugh."

"I'm sorry," Maddie said, shaking her head and trying to stop. "It's just that I really love that movie too. I didn't want to say it because I thought for sure you'd laugh at me."

"I would never laugh at that." Savannah smiled, secretly thrilled to find out they had the same favorite movie. "You should probably know something about hockey too. You said you weren't much of a fan, right?"

"Well, I've been reading a lot about it, and I've watched some games on the internet." Maddie seemed embarrassed to admit to it, but Savannah found it rather endearing to learn she was willing to go to all the trouble to pick up hockey knowledge on her own. "I know all about the penalties, but there's one thing I haven't run across."

"What's that?"

"The jersey you wear has a C on it. I know it stands for captain, I'm not that naïve," Maddie said with a grin. "But in the games I watched, there were players who had an A on their jerseys. Does that mean they're assistant captains?"

"It means alternate captain. The captain and alternates are the only ones who can speak to the officials about calls made on the ice. There are alternates in case the captain isn't available due to injury or if they're already in the penalty box. For that reason, you don't usually find the alternates on the same line as the captain."

It had been a long time since she'd needed to explain hockey to a woman, mostly because the women she spent time with couldn't care less about hockey. Either that or they were already fans and didn't need any explanations. It was nice sitting here on a lazy Saturday afternoon talking hockey with Maddie.

"You must make a pretty good living at it, right?"

"Are you a gold digger?" Savannah narrowed her eyes at her. "Just after my vast fortune?"

"I wouldn't care if a woman had any money at all as long as she was a good person and made me laugh." Maddie said, sounding and looking completely serious.

"Good answer," Savannah replied with a nod. In fact it was the best reaction she could have hoped for. "Actually, no, I don't make enough playing hockey to even live on. I'm a veterinarian during the day. Well, during the season I'm on call and only go in for a couple of days a week. In the off-season, I work there full time. The woman I work for is pretty flexible with me because she knows hockey is my first passion, and she also knows I won't be playing forever, so someday she'll get me full-time all year."

"That's nice."

"Tell me about your photography."

"It took me a long time to get to where I am now, which is working for myself." Maddie put their garbage back in the backpack and took another drink of her water. "I started out working for a newspaper, and then a couple of magazines, but now I make a pretty good living doing things like publicity stills, which I'm doing for the Warriors, and I also did for the orchestra in Chicago. Once a year I travel to different places and take photos of nature, which I sell to magazines and as art."

"Very cool." Savannah always wanted to travel somewhere other than the United States and Canada. Maybe someday she could go somewhere with Maddie.

Damn it, she really needed to stop thinking this way. She needed to remind herself that even though they were dating, it wasn't real. Even if she'd wanted to date her for real, it would never work. Not to mention she wasn't sure Maddie would want to.

A group of hikers was headed their way, and their tranquil afternoon seemed to be coming to a close. Maddie stood and looked down at Savannah.

"Ready to go?" she asked, even though she'd be perfectly happy to sit here and talk to Savannah all day long. It wasn't realistic to think like that. She had a feeling it was going to be difficult to keep in mind they were only faking this relationship, especially if they had many more dates like this one.

"I guess." Savannah sounded reluctant to leave as well, which caused a surge of happiness to run wild through Maddie. Was it possible Savannah could be thinking the same things?

No, she told herself. Savannah was best friends with Kelly, who was so obviously a player, and that made the odds pretty good Savannah was as well. Especially given the descriptor of *perpetually single* Savannah had labeled herself. At best this was simply a fun diversion for Savannah, and Maddie knew she'd do well to remember it.

"What about convincing people we're together?" Maddie asked when they'd almost made it back to the parking area. "I mean, if we're supposed to be dating, we'd be kissing and touching, wouldn't we?"

Savannah didn't answer right away, and she was worried maybe she wouldn't. They got to Savannah's motorcycle and she was about to pose the question again when Savannah decided to respond.

"I think the more time we spend together, the easier it would be to make everyone believe we're dating," she said with a shrug before unhooking the helmets and handing one to Maddie. "The more comfortable we are with each other the more convincing we'll be, don't you think?"

"Maybe," Maddie answered as she put the helmet on and got on the bike behind her. "So maybe we shouldn't tell people until we get to that point."

"A good idea," Savannah said over her shoulder. She started the bike and Maddie put her arms around her, clasping her hands against Savannah's surprisingly firm stomach. Savannah placed a hand on top of hers. "Hold on tight."

That won't be a problem, Maddie thought. She had the urge to let her hands wander up and cover Savannah's breasts, but when they started to move, she was actually afraid to move them anywhere, and held on a little tighter.

She was very aware of her breasts pressed against Savannah's back, and Savannah's ass pushed back tightly between her legs. She felt the first signs of arousal and shifted slightly on the seat.

"You okay back there?" Savannah asked over her shoulder.

"Fine," Maddie replied, but she wasn't sure she would ever be fine again. All she could think about was being in this same position, sans clothes. No, reminding herself this was all fake wasn't going to be easy.

Chapter Ten

The next ten days or so flew by, and before Savannah knew it, Court and Lana had arrived in town for their wedding. Gail had asked her to pick them up from the airport, and Savannah was happy to oblige. She and Maddie hadn't spent a lot of time together since Savannah had been keeping fairly busy at the vet's office, not to mention Maddie stressing about shooting this wedding. Apparently, it was the first wedding she'd ever done, and she wanted it to go perfectly. Savannah hoped they'd be seeing more of each other once the nuptials were over.

"So, Van, are you bringing a date to the wedding?" Court asked as Savannah pulled her car into traffic leaving the airport

"What?" Savannah glanced at her out of the corner of her eye. "You know I don't date."

"Yeah, I do, but I was hoping you might have changed in the time I've been gone."

Courtney Abbott had played nine full seasons with the Kingsville Warriors, and for most of that time Savannah and Kelly had been her line mates. The three of them had spent a lot of time together on and off the ice, and other than Kelly, Court knew her best. When Court had been traded early on in her tenth season, Savannah and Kelly had both struggled at first learning to play with a new center as well as losing their best friend.

But happiness looked good on Court, and on Lana, the woman she was going to marry. Court was now the assistant coach for the Wolves, the women's team in Chicago, and was on track to take over as head coach when the woman currently in the position retired after the next season.

"I am sort of seeing someone," Savannah said, and almost instantly regretted it. Court turned her head and gave Lana a strange look. She saw Lana shrug when she glanced at her in the rearview mirror.

"How do you *sort of* see someone?" Eric, Lana's eighteen-year-old son, asked from the back seat where he was sitting next to his mother. Eric was a pretty incredible hockey player himself, having led his junior team to two straight Memorial Cup titles. He'd been taken by the Chicago Blackhawks late in the first round of the NHL Entry Draft just the month before.

"It's kind of complicated," Savannah said with a sigh.

"I think we need to hear this story," Lana said.

"Later, okay?" Savannah looked at Eric in the mirror and, without giving anyone a chance to respond, addressed him. "So, Eric, I guess you're probably pretty excited to be in the Blackhawks organization."

"They're my favorite team, so yeah," he said with a grin. "But Philadelphia or New York would have been okay too, because it would be close to my grandparents. My uncle Joey has promised to bring them to my first game in the NHL though, so that's pretty cool."

"The Flyers are my team," Savannah told him with a grin of her own. "Even though they've pretty well sucked for the past few years. Where am I taking you guys?"

"Lana and Eric are staying with her parents, and I'm staying with Lori," Court said, referring to her younger sister.

"You're not staying together somewhere?"

"My parents are old-fashioned," Lana said

"Don't they know you live together?" Savannah asked.

"They do, but they won't allow it in their house," Eric said with a chuckle.

Lana leaned forward and placed a hand on Court's shoulder, giving it a squeeze. "It will be good for Court to spend some time with her friends since she doesn't get the chance to see you guys very often."

"You wouldn't say that if you knew us better," Savannah said with a wink directed at Court.

Maddie was nervous as hell. She'd made the trip to Lana's parents' house a few days earlier so Maria Caruso could give her a tour and let her see where the wedding was going to take place. She'd never photographed a wedding before, and because it was such a huge event for any couple, she was afraid she was going to screw everything up. The yard was a good size, but considering the entire Warriors team was invited, along with people from Chicago and former Olympic teammates of Court's, not to mention Lana's extended family, she was worried there wasn't going to be enough room. But, she told herself, it wasn't really her problem. All she needed was room to set up her equipment, and some decent sunlight to take her photos.

She was busy going over her list of things she needed for the wedding when her phone began to ring. Exasperated, she got up to retrieve it from the kitchen counter where she'd left it earlier. She smiled when she saw it was Lana calling.

"Hey, lady, I guess you made it here all right?" she said when she answered.

"Yes, safe and sound," Lana said. "Savannah Wells picked us up at the airport and just dropped Eric and me off at my parents."

"Did you leave Court at home?" Maddie joked.

"Yeah, I decided to marry someone else." Lana laughed, and Maddie laughed along with her. "My parents won't let her stay here with me, so she's staying at her sister's house until the wedding."

"That's a little odd, isn't it?"

"Not if you knew my parents," Lana said with a sigh. "Mom said you came by the other day. Does everything look satisfactory to you?"

"That's probably something you should ask the wedding planner, not the photographer." Maddie moved from where she'd been sitting at the kitchen table and settled in on the couch. It didn't take long for Duke, her three-year-old black German shepherd, to jump up and get comfortable with his head resting on her lap. She absently scratched behind his ear as she talked, and he sighed happily. "But everything seems fine for what I need."

Mary was the one who'd wanted the dog, but he bonded with Maddie, much to Mary's chagrin. So, when Maddie had decided to move to Kingsville to be closer to her sister, there really wasn't any question Duke would be going with her. He was nothing but a big cuddle-bug, which surprised Maddie, given the stigma so often associated with his breed.

"Do you miss Chicago?" Lana asked her.

"I don't, believe it or not," she answered, surprising herself. She hadn't really thought about Chicago much since she'd moved, and she'd loved the city. "I thought I would since Kingsville is such a small town in comparison, but I like it here. I do miss the Cubs though."

"Have you met anyone?"

Savannah's face popped into her mind, but she wasn't sure she wanted to talk about her quite yet. They were only pretending to date, after all. They hadn't discussed whether or not Savannah was going to tell Court, and since they were friends, Savannah wasn't sure she should bring it up with Lana.

"Sort of," she finally said. Lana chuckled, and Maddie sat up a little straighter. "What?"

"Nothing," Lana said. "It's just that Savannah told us she was *sort of* seeing someone. It isn't something you hear every day."

"No, I guess not." Maddie's pulse sped up at the thought of Savannah even remotely considering they were seeing each other.

Maddie had wanted to go knock on her door more than once since the hike they'd taken, but had somehow resisted. At least so far. The kiss they'd shared on the Fourth of July had fueled her dreams ever since.

They talked for a few more minutes, and then Lana had to go because her mother needed help with something in the kitchen. Maddie set the phone on the coffee table and sighed, causing Duke to lift his head and look at her with his soulful brown eyes.

"Sometimes I wish I was a dog, boy," she said to him. He thumped his tail and rested his chin on her leg again. "You've got it made not having to worry about relationships."

CHAPTER ELEVEN

S avannah wasn't sure she wanted to do this. Court and Lana had invited her to dinner and encouraged her to bring along the woman she was *sort of* seeing. Why the hell had she even let that little tidbit slip out of her mouth? And why was it when someone coupled up they instantly wanted all their friends to do it too?

She sighed and grabbed her keys off the counter before she could talk herself out of it. They were supposed to be dating, after all. No time like the present to get started. She walked up to Maddie's front door and raised her hand to knock, but stopped right before making contact. She turned around and looked out at the neighborhood.

When her girlfriend in college had dumped her, she'd sworn to herself she'd never give anyone else the chance to break her heart so thoroughly. Shauna had decided since Savannah was too busy with hockey and her veterinary studies to spend time with her, she'd find someone else to spend time with. And boy, did she. The last Savannah heard, she'd married the guy and they were living in California with their two kids.

The devastation she'd felt at the loss of the woman who had promised to love her forever and never hurt her almost cost her both of her careers. She'd locked herself away in her dorm room and refused to come out for weeks. Kelly was the only one she'd let in, and it was Kelly who'd talked her into rejoining the land of the living. It was then they'd set up their rules for "dating." And for the past ten years it had worked perfectly.

But now there was Maddie, living next door to her and managing to get under her skin like no one else ever had. She thought about her all the time, and really, that wasn't acceptable. She was refusing to go out when Kelly would invite her to the clubs, and she knew Kelly wouldn't put up with it much longer.

No, this was a bad idea. Pretending to date was going to lead to nothing but trouble, especially since Savannah already wanted to rip Maddie's clothes off every time she saw her. What good could possibly come from this situation? She made up her mind to walk away and go back home, but a dog inside the house began barking as soon as she took her first step away from the door. And then the door opened, causing her to turn back around, and she got lost in the beauty before her.

"Duke doesn't like it when people hang out on the porch," Maddie said, one hand firmly gripping the collar of a large black German shepherd.

If Savannah hadn't spent the better parts of her day with big dogs, she might be a little afraid of this one. He sat down next to Maddie's feet and watched Savannah, his tail wagging furiously. Obviously, like Leo, Duke was under the impression that anyone who came to the house was there to see him, and not Maddie.

"Duke, huh?" Savannah said, one eyebrow quirked. "Not a very original name. You wouldn't believe how many dogs named Duke I see in a given week."

"It's better than my second choice, which was just Dog."

"You really need to work on your name choosing ability."

"Don't make fun of his name," Maddie said, looking as serious as could be. "I might have to let him attack you."

"My guess is he'd knock me over and sit on my chest while he licked my face."

"Yeah, he probably would." Maddie laughed and stepped aside. "Come in before he decides to do it anyway and rips my arm off in the process."

"We wouldn't want that, would we, Duke?" Savannah walked past them into the house and waited for Maddie to shut the door. As soon as she let Duke go, he ran to her and sniffed her shoes, the tail never slowing at all. "To what do I owe the honor of your company this afternoon?"

"Court and Lana are in town," Savannah said.

"I know." Maddie led her into the kitchen and offered her a drink. After getting a glass of water for them both, they went to the living room and sat on the couch. "I talked to Lana this afternoon."

"Well, they invited me to dinner tonight, and they insisted I bring a date." Savannah silently chided herself, because obviously everything she'd decided on the porch a few minutes earlier just flew out the window when she was face-to-face to Maddie. And who could blame her, really? Maddie's short blond hair was stylishly messy, whether she'd intended it to look that way or not didn't matter. Savannah watched as Maddie ran a hand through it, a thoroughly sexy move in her opinion.

"That's interesting, because I was just about to call you and tell you the exact same thing."

"I'm not completely surprised," Savannah said, wondering if they somehow knew about them. She looked down at Duke, who was sitting on the floor but resting his chin on her thigh. "Did you tell Lana about what we're doing?"

"No." Maddie shook her head. "I figured we should talk about it before we tell anyone."

"Then I guess we should decide a few things."

"Okay."

"Are you sure you want to do this?"

"Are you changing your mind?" Maddie asked, leaning back into the corner of the couch and looking at her. Savannah shook her head, even though yes, she was. "And are we trying to fool everyone, or just Faith and Lisa?"

"I don't see why we can't tell Court and Lana the truth," Savannah said after some contemplation. Her first instinct was to say the latter, but she thought better of it. The less people who knew this wasn't a real relationship the better. Less chance for anyone to accidently slip in front of her moms.

"But we're going to lie to everyone else?" Maddie asked, sounding skeptical. "Even Kelly?"

"Especially Kelly," Savannah replied, chuckling softly. Maddie didn't know this, but Kelly was the worst at keeping secrets, especially from Lisa and Faith. "I think if she knew it was fake, she wouldn't be able to help herself. With you or Faith and Lisa."

"What do you mean?"

"She's the biggest flirt I know. She's always trying to come on to women, but I think if she knew we were together, she'd leave you alone." At least she hoped that would be the case. She'd never had a girlfriend to put the theory to the test. "If she knew it was fake, she'd probably flirt mercilessly with you, which would in turn give it away."

"Okay, then we probably won't get away with sitting this far apart." Maddie indicated the empty cushion on the couch separating them. "We'll have to hold hands and act like we have feelings for each other."

That won't be a problem, Savannah thought, and wondered where it had come from. It was no use denying it, at least to herself. She was incredibly attracted to Maddie, and she was beginning to worry spending time together was going to be more difficult for her than it would be for Maddie.

"Should we try it?" Maddie asked, and Savannah forced herself to stay put while Maddie moved close enough for their thighs to touch. She took Savannah's hand and entwined their fingers before pulling it over to rest on her lap. Maddie's thumb gently caressed hers, and she felt a heat growing deep in her belly. She wanted to pull her hand away, but she couldn't. "This isn't so bad, is it?"

"No," Savannah said, her voice a bit hoarse. She cleared her throat and gave it another go. "No. It's the opposite of bad."

"Good," Maddie said before letting go of her hand and putting a few inches between them. "Be back here at six, and I'll drive us to Lana's."

Wait, what? Savannah looked at Maddie and wondered if she was really as unaffected by their closeness as she seemed to be. She was pretty sure there was a mutual attraction thing happening between them, but maybe she was reading things wrong. This really was going to suck if she was the only one feeling what she thought was a spark between them.

"Okay, I guess I'll see you at six," Savannah said as she started to stand. She stopped when Maddie put a hand on her arm.

"I didn't mean you had to leave right now," Maddie said. "Let's figure out what we're going to tell people, and when."

"I assume we're going to tell Court and Lana tonight." Savannah made the statement with the hint of a question in her voice, and Maddie nodded her agreement. "I guess we should probably tell my moms and Kelly soon, because I'm sure they'll be seeing Court before the wedding. Lisa and Faith love Court like she was one of their own. What about your sister? When will you tell her?"

"Probably this weekend, if it's okay with you," Maddie said. "Amy wants to come spend the night on Friday, so I figured I'd tell them then, or when I take her back home on Saturday."

"Should we do the big reveals together?" Savannah was worried they wouldn't be able to pull this off, but since Maddie had been so gracious in offering to help her out, she felt she deserved to have Savannah give it her all. And since she lived right next door, it would make sense for them to see each other on the weekend, right?

"It might be more convincing that way," Maddie said with a nod.

"Yeah, except for Kelly," Savannah said. Kelly would know they were lying if Maddie was there when she told her. "Kelly knows me too well. I think I could make it more believable if I told her on my own."

"Oh, okay," Maddie said, sounding a little disappointed, which was in total contradiction to the smile Savannah was sure was fake. It made her heart hurt to realize she'd disappointed her, and she silently vowed to never do it again.

"But if you want to be there, I'm sure we could make it work."

"You're sweet," Maddie said as she squeezed Savannah's knee and shook her head. "But you're probably right. It's fine for you to do it on your own."

"Okay, so when did we start dating?" Savannah knew it would be a question most people were going to ask, and it was best to be on the same page.

"The day after the carnival?" Maddie asked. "Since Lisa wanted me to ask you out, we could say I did it that night, and we had our first official date the next evening."

"Perfect," Savannah said with a nod. For the first time, she was thinking this could really work. She just needed to keep reminding herself it wasn't real, even though they'd be trying hard to convince everyone else it was.

Chapter Twelve

Savannah shifted her weight nervously from foot to foot as they stood on the Carusos' front porch waiting for someone to answer the door. She felt incredibly nervous about this, but had no idea why. They weren't going to lie to Court and Lana, so there was no reason for any nervousness.

"It's a good thing we aren't going to lie to them," Maddie said quietly. "I'm beginning to think you might not be able to pull it off if you're this anxious now."

"I'll be fine when it comes time to tell other people," she said, sounding brusque to her own ears. She sighed and looked at Maddie. "I'm sorry. That was uncalled for. I think I'm a bit edgy because these are the first people we're even mentioning this to. I'll be fine this weekend when we tell our families."

Maddie looked unconvinced but didn't say anything in response. Savannah took her hand and smiled at her, and Maddie seemed to relax a bit. She had no idea she was making Maddie tense by her own actions. She took a deep breath to calm herself just as the door opened, and they were face to face with Lana.

Lana smiled but looked confused. Understanding seemed to dawn on her when her gaze focused on their hands which were still clasped. Savannah tried to let go, but Maddie tightened her grip slightly.

"Is it Savannah or Maddie?" she heard Court call from somewhere in the house behind Lana.

"Yes," Lana called back.

"Sorry, honey, but that isn't really an answer," Court said as she emerged from the kitchen and walked up behind Lana. She noticed their hands right away, and a big smile broke out and she looked at Savannah. "Okay, wait. This is who you're *sort of* seeing?"

"And this is who you're *sort of* seeing?" Lana asked Maddie.

"This is a story I need to hear," Court said, grabbing Savannah by the bicep and pulling her into the house.

"Indeed," Lana said. She stepped aside for Maddie to enter, and they all went straight to the living room.

"Is it your friends?" came a voice from the kitchen. Savannah assumed it was Lana's mother.

"Yes it is, Mom," Lana called back.

"Dinner will be ready in about twenty minutes."

"Then you better make this quick," Court said, the interest obvious in her expression. She motioned for Savannah to start explaining.

"Well, you know Lisa," Savannah said to Court, but then she looked at Lana. "You don't, but I have a feeling you will."

They spent the next fifteen minutes or so explaining the reasons behind what they were doing, and Court and Lana were just looking at them like they couldn't believe what they were hearing. Savannah leaned back on the couch and looked at Maddie, who simply shrugged. She seemed to be just as surprised at Court and Lana being rendered speechless.

"Mom," Eric said as he walked into the room. He stopped abruptly when he must have sensed the seriousness of their conversation. He walked backward out of the room. "Sorry."

"It's a good thing you two are dating," Lana said with a smirk, making air quotes around the word dating. "Otherwise Eric would have no doubt tried to get you together."

"Yeah, he did it with us," Court said with a laugh. She ran a hand through her hair and stared at Savannah. "Have you told Kelly you're dating?"

"Not yet," Savannah replied.

"We invited her tonight, but she said she was busy," Court said. "How are you ever going to convince her this is real? Are you ready to give up clubbing with her? I mean, she knows you better than anyone. If she sees you chatting up other women, she'll know this isn't real."

Maddie looked at Savannah, her heart sinking a little to realize her fears about Savannah being a player were just confirmed. Savannah looked at her nervously, but refused to meet her eyes. She felt Lana's eyes on her, no doubt realizing Savannah hadn't told Maddie about her lifestyle.

"Court was the same way when we met," Lana said to Maddie.

"And after we met, I completely changed my ways," Court added.

"Yeah, well, this isn't real, so she doesn't have to change her ways," Maddie said, even though it made her heart hurt to say the words. In reality, she had no right to think Savannah wouldn't see anyone else while they were doing this. Savannah looked at her, and she forced a smile. "It's not a big deal."

"Are you sure about that?" Lana asked, and Maddie saw out of the corner of her eye when Savannah turned her head and looked at her, presumably waiting for her answer.

"Of course," Maddie said, her voice breaking. She shook her head and stood. "Excuse me for a moment. I need to use the restroom before dinner."

She walked out of the room and was totally aware of the silence following her. She was sure they were all watching her. What Court had said shouldn't be causing this reaction in her. She was pretty sure it was jealousy, and she wasn't very in tune with that side of herself. She'd never felt jealousy before. She quickly learned she didn't much care for it.

"Hey, Maddie," Eric said as he walked up behind her when she turned down the hall toward the bathroom. She turned to face him and smiled. He was a wonderful young man. He enveloped her in a hug. "It's really good to see you again. How do you like it here in Kingsville?"

"It's okay," she said with a nod. "Hey, congratulations by the way. Your mom told me you were drafted in the first round last month. You must be pretty excited."

"I am," he said, looking embarrassed as he glanced down at his feet. "I'm not expecting to make the team this year, but maybe next year."

"You never know. You must be pretty good to be taken so early in the draft."

"I guess." He smiled as he met her eyes. "So…are you dating Savannah?"

Maddie wasn't sure what to say in response to his unexpected question. She looked toward the living room for a moment before turning back to him. She made a quick decision based on what she knew about him. He'd always been more mature than his age.

"It's complicated, but yes, we are dating."

"Awesome. I don't know her very well, but she's one of Court's best friends, so she must be a good person."

Maddie nodded before continuing her trek to the bathroom. She needed a moment to compose herself and to reconcile the fact she and Savannah would never be more than fake girlfriends to each other.

"Don't play with her," Lana said when Maddie was out of earshot. Savannah just looked at her in surprise. She didn't know Lana very well, but it was obvious she was serious. She knew instinctively it would be a bad idea to cross Lana Caruso. "I mean it, Savannah, she's been through a lot in the past six months or so."

"I would never hurt her," Savannah said, meaning every word.

"Is there any chance this could turn into something?" Lana asked.

Savannah wanted to say no, but she wasn't sure. Not one hundred percent, anyway. She looked at Court, pleading with her eyes for Court to help her out here. Court just shook her head and looked away. Obviously, she was on her own. She met Lana's gaze.

"I guess there's always a possibility, isn't there? I'm not so sure she wants it to turn into something though."

"Yeah, I wouldn't count on it," Lana said with a shake of her head. "As long as you both know what you're getting yourselves into, I should just back off. You're both adults, right?"

Lana got to her feet and went to the kitchen without another word. Court chuckled, causing Savannah to redirect her attention.

"Lana doesn't like games," Court said, shaking her head. "This seems like a game to her."

"But it's a game we're playing together, not against each other," Savannah said. "Trust me, I don't like games either. We've talked about this quite a bit, and we do know what we're doing."

"I believe you, Van." Court stood when Lana's mother announced dinner was ready. "Like Lana said, you're both adults. I just hope neither one of you gets hurt in the process."

"Me too." Savannah sighed, wondering if she should tell Court about the reservations she had concerning getting involved with someone. What would be the point though, really? It wasn't like they were on the verge of being any more than friends. Maybe if it looked as if they were going to move in another direction she'd call Court and seek her advice. Until then, she needed to concentrate on making sure she remembered they were only friends. But damn it, she wanted more, and the realization scared her half to death.

Dinner was filled with talk of the weather and where Court and Lana were going on their honeymoon. Hawaii sounded really nice to Savannah, and apparently to Maddie too, who was asking all kinds of questions about where they were staying, what they were planning to do, and how long they'd be there. Savannah thought her excitement was pretty cute and she couldn't help smiling at her enthusiasm.

Maddie invited her in after they got home, and although Savannah worried she was getting dangerously closer to crossing a line in their fake relationship, she accepted. They made themselves comfortable on the couch after Maddie took care of Duke and brought them both a bottle of water.

"I'm confused about something," Maddie said after a moment of silence. Savannah noticed she avoided meeting her gaze as she spoke.

"And what's that?"

"Court made mention of you picking up women. It sounded like it was probably a regular occurrence, but I haven't noticed you going out since I moved in here. It's not a bad thing, mind you, I used to live that life myself. I'm just wondering why you haven't been out with Kelly since we met."

Because it's you I want.

Those were the words on the tip of Savannah's tongue, but she somehow resisted blurting them out. She decided to downplay it, hoping she wouldn't alienate Maddie.

"I've been really busy," she said, and Maddie finally looked at her. She shrugged. "Between the vet's office and spending time with you, there just isn't any time. Or desire to, if I'm being honest."

Shit, shit, shit. No doubt Maddie would want an explanation of the last part of her statement. Savannah tried really hard to not react to the words slipping out without much thought and mentally crossed her fingers for Maddie to let it go.

"Oh. So you've been too tired?"

"Yeah," Savannah said, feeling as though she may have dodged a bullet. "Yeah, too tired. The closest bar to meet other lesbians is almost an hour away."

"You know you can though, right?" Maddie asked. "You don't have to change your life just because we're fake dating."

"Court was right," Savannah said, shaking her head. "Kelly would never believe we're dating if I went out with her and had some other woman coming on to me. She knows how I feel about cheating. She knows I'd never do it."

"Well, if you want to go out, you know, to dance or just to hang out with Kelly, maybe I could tag along. You know, so she wouldn't question our status."

Savannah nodded slowly, not sure she really liked the idea much. But, strangely, the more she mulled it over in her mind, the more it made sense. As long as they didn't dance to any slow songs, it would probably go a long way to convincing Kelly they were really together.

"Yeah, that might be a good idea."

Or it could end up being a really bad idea. Savannah prayed it wouldn't go horribly wrong.

CHAPTER THIRTEEN

Maddie opened the door to Savannah on Friday evening only a few minutes before Dana was due to arrive with Amy. She was going to tell Dana tonight, because Savannah had invited her and Amy to have brunch with Lisa and Faith the next morning. It wouldn't be good for her niece to find out she was dating Savannah before her own sister did.

Why had she agreed to let Amy spend the night tonight? Court and Lana's wedding was only four days away, and she was still stressing about the fear of screwing the whole day up for them by taking bad pictures. Of course deep down she knew she wouldn't, but because it was her first wedding shoot, the worry was unrelenting.

"I hope you didn't make solid plans for what to do with Amy this evening," Savannah said as she walked in. When Maddie turned around after shutting the door, she found herself incredibly close to her. Savannah had a huge grin on her face.

"You seem to be in a good mood," Maddie said. Savannah took her by the hand and led her into the living room. Once they were seated, Maddie decided she couldn't wait any longer. "Why are you in such a good mood?"

"Well, Amy is a big Warriors fan, right?"

"The biggest."

"Yeah, so I've arranged for a few members of the team, and Court and Eric too, to meet us at the arena tonight for a skating session."

"A what?" Maddie felt the color drain from her face. She'd never learned how to skate, and the thought of making a fool of herself in front of Savannah's friends and teammates held zero appeal to her. "I can't skate."

"What?" Savannah appeared genuinely surprised. "Who doesn't know how to skate?"

"I'd be willing to bet there are a hell of a lot of people who don't know how to skate," Maddie said. She shook her head, knowing this was an amazingly thoughtful thing for Savannah to do for Amy. "I'll be happy to sit in the stands and watch. Amy will love it."

"Oh, no," Savannah lifted Maddie's hand and placed a kiss on her knuckles, causing a flutter in Maddie's chest which only intensified when Savannah winked at her. "You're going to learn how to skate tonight."

"No." Maddie shook her head emphatically. "Just...no."

"The place is closed to the public tonight, so it's only going to be a few people," Savannah said, and much to her surprise, Maddie was beginning to warm up to the idea. "I promise I won't let you fall."

"Did you arrange to have it closed for tonight?"

"I did. People tend to get a little crazy when we show up somewhere in a group." Savannah sat back and released her hand, and Maddie wanted to snatch it back. "And with Court there, and a newly drafted future NHL star, closing the place seemed to be a logical decision."

"It must have cost you a fortune. Especially for a Friday night."

"Nah, it was nothing. It's not like there's a ton of people going ice skating in the middle of summer anyway." Savannah was smiling, and she sat up straight as she reached for Maddie's hand again. "A real girlfriend would want to do something like this, wouldn't she?"

"Yes." Maddie just looked at her, not knowing what else to say. If she wasn't careful, she might start to think of Savannah as a *real* girlfriend, and she had the feeling that would be a bad idea. Luckily, the doorbell rang then, and she didn't have to think of anything else to say. It was time to start convincing people they were dating. "That'll be Dana and Amy."

Savannah looked nervous, but she was obviously trying to cover it up by smiling a little too much. It was adorable. Maddie went to the door while Savannah stayed on the couch, trying to look casual and relaxed. Maddie chuckled to herself before letting her sister in.

"Are you sure you're all right with her staying the night?" Dana asked as they entered the house. "She can be a bit of a handful sometimes."

"Of course. Actually, Savannah's here, and she has a bit of a surprise for Amy."

"No way," Amy said as she leaned to the right to peer past Maddie into the living room. She dropped her overnight bag at her feet and started heading in Savannah's direction.

"Shoes, Amy," Dana said.

"It's all right," Maddie assured her. Dana was one of those people, but Maddie definitely wasn't. "Come say hi."

"You seem different," Dana said as they walked. "Are you okay?"

"I'm better than okay," Maddie said, sounding more confident than she felt. "I have something to tell you."

"Are you sick?" Dana could be such a drama queen sometimes.

"No." Maddie shook her head and rolled her eyes. She sat next to Savannah and reached for her hand. When she looked at her sister, she saw Dana's gaze was on their hands and there was a smirk on her face. "Savannah and I are dating."

"Each other?" Amy asked.

"Duh," Dana said, causing them all to laugh. She looked at Maddie and smiled. "When did this start?"

Maddie was relieved they'd ironed this detail out. She hadn't really expected the question to be the first one someone would ask, but evidently she was wrong. She met Savannah's eyes for a fraction of a second before Savannah decided to answer the question herself.

"She asked me to have dinner with her the night after the Fourth." Savannah squeezed her hand before holding it up in the air. "And we've been together ever since. I have to admit I'm glad I said yes to the date."

Maddie knew the smile on her face was a bit goofy, but she couldn't help it. Even the scowl on Dana's face couldn't erase it.

"You've been dating for almost three weeks and haven't told me?" Dana asked. Maddie knew she wasn't really mad, but she probably was a little hurt. "We tell each other everything, Mads."

"It was my fault," Savannah said, and Maddie felt incredibly happy to learn she was willing to protect her. "I wanted to wait to tell people. In Maddie's defense, she wanted to tell you right away, but I begged her not to. I didn't want to jinx it."

"Oh my," Dana said, placing a hand over her heart and tilting her head a bit. "Maddie, she's a keeper. Don't let her go."

"I'm not planning on it." Maddie hoped she sounded convincing enough, but not so much as to send Savannah running for the hills.

"So was this my surprise?" Amy asked, sounding a bit let down.

Maddie sighed. Amy was definitely a material girl, so she knew Amy had been expecting something she could hold in her hands. Maddie knew she could blame her sister and brother-in-law for that. They gave her pretty much everything she wanted. They hadn't grown up with much, so she had a feeling Dana was trying to make up for the way they were raised.

"No, it isn't," Maddie said. She looked at Savannah, wanting to give her the opportunity to become even more impressive in Amy's eyes.

"Do you ice skate?" Savannah asked, and Amy nodded a little too enthusiastically. "How would you like to go skating with some of the Warriors players tonight?"

"Seriously?" Amy asked, her eyes wide.

"Yep," Savannah said, looking rather pleased with herself. "Oh, and Courtney Abbott will be there too, along with her soon to be stepson, Eric Caruso."

"No way!" Amy got up and started jumping up and down in her excitement. "Eric is soooo dreamy."

"He's also too old for you," Dana said. "I think her crush on him has overtaken the one she has on you, Savannah."

"I'm devastated," Savannah said with a wink.

"Wait a minute," Dana said, a hand on Maddie's leg. "You don't know how to skate."

"Thanks for that," Maddie answered with another roll of her eyes. "I'm just going to watch."

"Think again," Savannah said.

"Okay, before you two get into a lovers' quarrel, I'm going to go home." Dana stood and hugged Amy good-bye. She then looked at Maddie and Savannah and shook her head. "I'm really happy for you guys. You're so cute together."

"All right, let's eat some dinner before we go," Maddie said after Dana was gone. "I have a feeling I'm going to need some fuel for this evening."

Chapter Fourteen

M addie hadn't been exaggerating—she really didn't know how to ice skate. As soon as her blade hit the ice for the first time, her arms started to windmill, and Savannah had to react quickly in order to stop her from falling on her ass. Somehow she managed not to laugh, which she was sure would have been a bad thing to do. Maddie was nervous enough about this without her feeling as though Savannah was making fun of her.

"Nice save, Wells," Charlotte Greene, their goaltender said as she skated past. "Are you looking to take my job?"

"Damn right I am," Savannah yelled after her. She placed an arm around Maddie's waist to help steady her, but Maddie reached out for the boards surrounding the rink. "You're doing fine."

"The hell I am," Maddie said, still reaching. "Get me over there or I'm taking you down with me."

Savannah got her close enough so she could grab onto the board, but once she had hold of it, Maddie visibly relaxed before her legs started sliding in different directions. Savannah grabbed her by placing her hands on Maddie's hips in order to keep her upright.

"This is stupid," Maddie said, leaning back slightly so their bodies were touching. "Just let me sit down and watch."

"Nobody would believe I'd date someone who wouldn't at least try to learn how to skate," Savannah said, her mouth just inches from Maddie's ear. She closed her eyes momentarily and breathed in the scent of her coconut shampoo. She managed to stop herself just before her lips touched Maddie's neck. She took a step back but let her hands stay on Maddie's hips until she was sure she wasn't going to fall if she let go.

"Then go skate," Maddie said, sounding seriously exasperated. "Let me just hang on and I'll work my way around the rink. Maybe I'll make it back here before everyone is ready to leave."

"You're kind of cute when you're mad," Savannah said with a chuckle.

"Oh great, so now you'll want to keep me mad all the time." Maddie had a death grip on the boards, and Savannah saw her knuckles were going white. She stepped closer again for just a moment.

"No, I won't," she said. "Because you're beautiful when you're happy."

Savannah quickly skated away, because she couldn't believe she'd just said those words out loud. What the hell was she thinking? She glanced back at Maddie and saw she was watching her with a perplexed look on her face. Just as she was turning her head back, she ran right into Eric and fell hard on her ass. He laughed as he reached a hand out to help her up. God, how freaking embarrassing.

"Are you all right?" he asked, obviously struggling to keep the grin off his face. She glared at him as she regained her feet.

"Laugh it up," she said, nodding her head. She gave him a playful shove.

"Careful, you might fall again," he said, a hand on her elbow. "I could teach you how to skate if you need a few pointers."

"You're a jerk." Savannah wanted to be mad at him for teasing her, but she had to admit it was pretty funny. She was supposed to keep Maddie from falling, and then she went and did it on her own. "You think anybody caught that on video?"

"Oh yeah." He nodded and pointed at Lana, who was sitting in the stands with her cell phone pointing right at them. "My guess is it'll be viral within the next twenty minutes."

"Great." Savannah rolled her eyes and took off in Lana's direction. She stopped in the perfect spot to send ice in her direction. "You put that on the internet and I'll make sure you never make it to your honeymoon."

"I wasn't really recording." Lana laughed and put the phone in her pocket. "I only wanted to mess with you."

"Well, if anybody," she said, spreading her arms out to encompass the entire building, "puts it on the internet, my threat still stands."

"I'll make sure Court threatens everyone," Lana said with a wink. Savannah laughed, knowing there wasn't anyone there who would be afraid of Court. "Go tell your girlfriend to come over here. I want to talk to her about the wedding."

Savannah helped Maddie off the ice and could tell she was instantly in a better mood. She wasn't doing much better walking with her skates on than she was actually skating, and Savannah took off on the ice as soon as she sat down to remove them.

"You two looked pretty cozy there," Kelly said as she bumped Savannah's shoulder. Savannah hadn't even noticed her approaching.

"Just trying to teach her how to skate," Savannah said with a shrug.

"Yeah, right," Kelly said, shaking her head. "You don't have to have your arms around someone to teach them how to skate."

"You do if you're trying to keep them from falling on their ass."

"Then it's too bad she wasn't there to save you." Kelly smirked and started to pull away from her, but Savannah sped up to catch her, knowing she needed to tell her about dating Maddie. This was the one conversation she wasn't looking forward to. She grabbed Kelly by the arm and led her off the ice. "What the hell, Van?"

"I need to talk to you for a minute." They stood off to the side in case anyone else wanted off—or on—the ice, and Savannah raked a hand through her hair.

"Are you going to talk, or are you just going to stand there?"

"Maddie and I are dating." There. She said it. And now Kelly was just staring at her, a look of disbelief on her face. "Say something."

"What do you want me to say? On the Fourth, she told me she wasn't interested in dating because she'd just broken up with her girlfriend." Kelly was obviously a bit miffed, but whether it was directed at her or Maddie, Savannah couldn't tell. "I guess it was just me she wasn't interested in dating."

"You don't date," Savannah said, pointing out the obvious.

"No shit. Neither do you."

Savannah looked down at her feet. Maybe it was a mistake to try to fool Kelly. She'd never lied to her before, about anything. She was trying to convince herself of the reasons it would be bad to come clean when Kelly saved her the trouble.

"She must be pretty special," Kelly said with a glance over at Maddie and Lana. "I guess I always knew we'd have to grow up and stop living like tomcats, but I just never thought it would happen this soon."

Kelly put a hand on her shoulder and squeezed gently. Savannah looked at her and was surprised to see a smile on Kelly's face.

"If you're happy, then I'm happy for you, Van. But you better ask me to stand up for you at your wedding."

"Pretty sure that won't be happening anytime soon." Savannah chuckled and looked over at Maddie and Lana laughing. For just a moment, she wondered what it would be like to really be dating Maddie.

"Have you told her about Mary?" Lana asked as they sat watching the people skate.

"I just said she cheated on me and I needed to get away from her." Maddie sighed. Getting to know Savannah had been a nice distraction, but the worry about Mary showing up someday lingered in the back of her mind ever since Dana had asked if it was a possibility. "I didn't see any reason to tell her my ex is a psycho."

"Aren't you worried she might show up and cause problems?" Lana looked at her with obvious concern. "She could hurt someone."

"She was obsessive and verbally abusive. I doubt she'd actually physically hurt anyone."

"But you don't really know that for sure." Lana glanced out at the ice for a moment. "Escalation isn't out of the question for people like her."

"She knows Dana lives here, but I think I was pretty convincing when I told her we didn't get along. I doubt she'll think I moved here." Maddie wasn't entirely sure who she was trying to convince. It wasn't as though she hadn't considered the things Lana was saying. "And if she does show up and finds out I'm dating someone, maybe she'll give up."

"Yeah, right," Lana said sarcastically. "I think you should warn Savannah at the very least. I think she really likes you."

"You don't know what you're talking about," Maddie said with a quick shake of her head. "It's fake. It's just to convince her mom to stop setting her up on blind dates."

"Yeah, I know what you guys told us the other night, but Court says there's something different about Savannah when she talks about you. When she's with you." Lana nodded at the same time Maddie was shaking her head. "Court knows her better than either one of us, and I believe her."

"She's perpetually single. Her words, not mine." Maddie risked a glance toward Savannah and Kelly who were talking just off the ice. Kelly put a hand on Savannah's shoulder and said something that caused Savannah to smile just before she looked in their direction. Maddie laughed and turned her attention back to Lana. "It's a pleasant thought, but it's never going to turn into something more than it is."

"And I thought when I went back to Chicago I'd never see Court again," Lana said. "Yet look where we are now."

Maddie didn't know what to say. She'd read romance novels before about people in fake relationships, and they pretty much always ended up falling in love with each other by the end of the book. Was it possible it could happen to them? No, she thought as she shook her head. Those stories were fiction, and this was real life. It was more likely they'd end up at each other's throats if Savannah was really determined to stay single.

Still, it was an intriguing thought.

Chapter Fifteen

The look on Lisa's face when she walked in with Maddie and Amy for brunch the next day was priceless. She didn't even give them a chance to say a word before she clapped and laughed with unbridled joy. Savannah laughed as Lisa called out for Faith.

"Faith, honey," Lisa said, off to find her. "We have a wedding to plan."

"Christ," Savannah said under her breath. She gave an apologetic look to Maddie and started to walk away to put an end to the wedding plans when she felt Maddie grab her hand. "She's going a little overboard."

"Let her," Maddie said with a smile. "She's happy, so just give her a moment."

Savannah was a little shocked when Maddie leaned closer and kissed her on the lips. In an instant, everyone else in the house ceased to exist, even Amy, who was standing right next to them, watching. Maddie put a hand on Savannah's chest above her breasts and pushed gently when Savannah tried to capture her lips again.

"Later," she said with a tilt of her head toward Amy, and toward Lisa and Faith as well, who were standing a few feet away beaming. Savannah cleared her throat.

"No wedding plans," she said, glaring at both of them.

"Yet," Amy said with a grin, causing both Savannah and Maddie to look at her in shock. "But they're so cute together, aren't they?"

"More than cute," Lisa said, looking at Savannah. "I knew I could set you up with the perfect woman."

"Wait, what?" Faith asked. "You set them up?"

"I convinced Madison to ask her out, and now look!" Lisa clapped her hands together again.

"Sometimes I think you're still a teenager, Lisa," Faith said, laughing.

"Just young at heart," Lisa said with a playful shove.

"Okay, let's eat," Savannah said, wondering if this had been such a good idea after all. She hadn't really expected Lisa to start in on wedding talk right away. She walked past everyone into the kitchen but stopped when she realized the table wasn't even set yet. "What's going on, Lisa, are you slacking?"

"Just sit down and tell us all about what's been going on between the two of you," Lisa said, bustling past Savannah to pull an egg and ham casserole out of the oven. When she looked back at them, no one had moved. "Sit! Faith, set the table for me, please."

"I'm sorry about this," Savannah said, leaning close to Maddie after they'd taken their seats.

"For what?" Maddie looked to be genuinely perplexed.

"Um, the wedding comment?" Savannah laughed and shook her head. "I didn't expect her to run with that quite so fast."

"So?" Lisa said once they were all seated at the table. She put food on her plate and passed the dish to Maddie. "Tell us everything."

"I really don't like to kiss and tell," Maddie said with a grin and a wink directed toward Savannah. Savannah shook her head, impressed with her effort of trying to derail Lisa's line of questioning, but she knew Lisa wouldn't let it go.

"It's okay, dear, you don't have to," Faith said. "Vanna tells us everything."

"Vanna?" Maddie asked, looking at Savannah.

"Faith, I would kick you under the table if I wasn't worried I'd miss and hit someone else," Savannah said, giving her a warning glare. Of course, Faith simply laughed at her.

"I only call her that because she hates it," Faith said to Maddie. "I've always loved to push her buttons."

"So, training camp opens up in about a month," Savannah said, handing the dish off to Amy. She didn't think the subject change would work, but she could hope.

"Hey, since you two are dating, does that mean I get free tickets to the games?" Amy asked, a hopeful grin on her face.

"Amy," Maddie said, her tone a definite warning.

"What?" she asked, all innocence. "You'll never get what you want if you don't ask for it."

"She's got a point," Lisa said.

"I think we could probably arrange something for you," Savannah said to Amy.

"You don't have to do that," Maddie said.

"It's not a big deal," Savannah said with a shrug. "They allot each player two tickets per game, and while I usually give mine to Faith and Lisa, Kelly gives hers away to any player who needs extras. So, I may not be able to get you tickets to every game, but I probably could for a lot of them."

"Cool," Amy said before shoving a bite of food into her mouth.

"Why doesn't Kelly use hers?" Maddie asked, and Savannah realized she'd never told her Kelly's story.

"Kelly's parents were killed in a car accident when she was fifteen," Faith said with a sigh. "There was a lot of red tape to go through, but she eventually ended up living here with us until she and Savannah went off to college. She has no other family to speak of."

"Wow, so she's like part of the family." Maddie put her hand over Savannah's which was resting on the table.

"I've always thought of her as a sister as well as my best friend," Savannah said with a nod. She looked down at their hands and wondered at the warm feeling she got in the pit of her stomach from the simple gesture.

"So, about those wedding plans," Lisa said after a moment. Savannah knew the subject change was too good to be true.

❖

Luckily, they managed to leave not long after they finished eating, using the excuse of needing to get Amy home. Savannah was able to somehow sidetrack Lisa every time she tried to get them to talk about *them.*

They were on their way back home after dropping Amy off when Savannah's phone began to ring. She was surprised to see it was Gail calling. Why would she be calling during the off-season, she wondered. Luckily, Maddie was driving, so she didn't hesitate to answer.

"What's up, Coach?"

"I'm sorry to call you out of the blue like this, Wells," Gail said, not surprisingly using her last name as she would during the season. It wasn't like they were friends away from the game. "I need to go out of town, and I won't be back before next weekend. My sister is having a baby."

"Okay," Savannah said, not quite understanding. "Congratulations. Are you sure it's me you meant to call?"

"Yes, I'm sure," Gail said with a chuckle. "Court's wedding is Tuesday. I won't be able to be there."

"Oh, shit," Savannah said with a quick glance at Maddie. "No, you can't do this to me."

Savannah had completely forgotten Court set up a contingency plan. If, for some reason, Gail couldn't be at the wedding, Savannah was supposed to take over and stand up with Court. This was definitely not something she was expecting to happen, but obviously Court knew it had been a possibility.

"Technically, it's my sister who's doing it to you, not me. She went into labor this morning, two weeks early, I might add, and I need to fly down to Georgia. My plane leaves in an hour."

"Does Court know?"

"I was hoping you could tell her. I really won't have time to call her until after I land, but I wanted to make sure I gave you a heads-up. She knew this could happen, so I'm sure she won't be completely shocked."

"That makes one of us then." Savannah closed her eyes and leaned her head against the headrest. "Have a safe flight. I'll let Court know."

"Thanks, Wells."

Savannah sat there staring at her phone after they disconnected. She didn't want to be part of the wedding. She just wanted to go and watch, and have a good time at the reception. Now she actually had to work. And give a speech. *Fuck.*

"Is everything okay?" Maddie asked after a moment.

"No."

"You want to talk about it?"

"That was Gail Crawford. The woman who sold you the house. She's also the head coach of the Warriors, and Court's best friend." Savannah shoved the phone back in her pocket and sighed loudly. "She was supposed to stand with Court at the wedding, but her sister has shit timing and decided to have her baby two weeks early. So now it falls on me to be at Court's side when she marries Lana."

"And that's a problem why, exactly?"

"I really don't like crowds."

"Seriously?" Maddie laughed but sobered quickly when she glared at her. "You perform in front of crowds all the time."

"Yeah, playing a game I've been playing all my life," Savannah said. "Which is a lot different from standing in front of people and giving a speech."

"I'm sure you'll do fine."

"Right." Savannah snorted. "Okay, change of plans. I need you to take me to Court's sister's house so I can tell her what's going on."

Chapter Sixteen

"You look more nervous than I feel," Court said as they were getting ready in the spare bedroom of Lana's parents' house. The wedding was going to start in less than an hour.

"You could call it off and spare me," Savannah said, only half joking. Her stomach was strangely queasy.

"Not a chance." Court laughed and clapped her on the back. "I was lucky enough to find the love of my life, and I am not letting her get away."

"Some friend you are." Savannah looked at herself in the mirror once Court finished helping her with her tie. The tux had been tailored to fit her perfectly, and she had to admit she looked pretty damn good. A knock on the door caused them both to jump before Court went and pulled it open.

"I wanted to get a few pictures of you outside before the ceremony," Maddie said as she fiddled with the camera. When she looked up and saw Savannah, her eyes went wide. Savannah walked over to them and couldn't help but smile. "Wow. You look...I mean, you *both* look amazing."

"We'll be down in just a minute," Court said, but Maddie seemed to be rooted to her spot, her eyes roaming Savannah's body. Court cleared her throat and waved a hand in front of Maddie's face. "Hello? We'll be right down."

"Oh, yeah, okay," Maddie said, taking a step backward before turning and walking quickly down the stairs. Court shut the door and faced Savannah, a smirk on her face.

"What?" Savannah asked. "I can't help it if a woman finds me attractive."

"Attractive?" Court asked. "She was about five seconds away from ripping your clothes off, my friend."

"You don't know what you're talking about."

"Maybe not, but I do know you." Court grabbed a rose to put in her lapel and then did the same for Savannah. "And you were about three seconds away from letting her."

Savannah wanted to argue. She really did. But she couldn't. Court knew her too well. She'd spent a lot of time with Maddie over the past few days, and she was confused by the thoughts and feelings she was experiencing. She'd lived the past ten years happy with her decision of never dating anyone seriously, but then along came Maddie who, in the span of just about three weeks, was seriously testing the theory.

"It's okay, Van," Court said, her hands on Savannah's shoulders. "You know you don't have to spend the rest of your life alone. I see the way the two of you look at each other. Maybe it's just lust, or maybe it's something more, but I think you might owe it to her, and yourself, to find out. You might just realize being with someone is so much better than being alone."

Maddie somehow managed to take the photos of Court and Savannah without drooling all over herself. The ones she took of just Court went much smoother. She couldn't take her eyes off Savannah in the black tux that fit her perfectly. She'd already taken the photos of Lana readying for her big day, and once the ceremony was over she'd take a few shots of the brides with their families.

"You look amazing today."

Maddie was setting up the tripod she would use to capture some key moments from the ceremony itself and hadn't noticed Savannah approaching. She stood up straight and looked down at the white slacks and blue blouse she was wearing. She'd considered buying a dress for the occasion, but she never felt comfortable in dresses or skirts.

"You clean up amazingly well yourself." Maddie reached out and brushed at Savannah's lapels, not able to help herself. She pretended to smooth out some nonexistent wrinkles just so she could keep touching her.

"This old thing?" Savannah laughed. "It's just something I threw on."

"Modest as well as devastatingly handsome," Maddie said with a nod of approval. "You're the whole package."

"So, do you have to work the entire day, or will you be able to kick your shoes off and celebrate with everyone later?" It was obvious Maddie's comment had embarrassed her by the slight reddening of her cheeks. Maddie found it adorable.

"I'll have to take a few photos at the reception, but I should be able to have some time to enjoy myself." Maddie looked around at the people in the yard, most of whom were sitting since the ceremony was set to take place in about five minutes. "Shouldn't you be up there with Court?"

"Probably," Savannah said as she walked backward a couple of steps. "Will you save a dance for me?"

Maddie nodded before waving her away. If she stayed there distracting her for much longer, not only would she never get her equipment ready in time, but she'd be sorely tempted to drag her into the house and have her way with her. And she was pretty sure even though Savannah was obviously attracted to her too, she didn't want things to go quite so far.

Yet, as Amy had said, but she'd been referring to a wedding. Maddie knew if she was ever going to break through Savannah's walls, it was going to take being slow and steady. Maddie was going to have to make Savannah think she couldn't live without her. The only problem was, she had no idea where to even start.

"Hey, beautiful," said a familiar voice from behind her. Maddie rolled her eyes before turning to face Kelly. She was sure Kelly was a great person—she was Savannah's best friend, after all—but she really didn't like the way she kept coming on to her. Especially now since Savannah had told her they were dating.

"Kelly," Maddie said in greeting. She gave her a perfunctory once-over. "You look nice."

"Thank you, as do you," she said with a wide smile. "Will you save me a dance at the reception?"

"I'll only be dancing with Savannah, but thank you for asking." Maddie turned back to her equipment, but it was obvious after a moment Kelly wasn't going anywhere. "Was there something else?"

"I'm just trying to figure out why you're dating her," Kelly said with a shrug. "I mean, don't get me wrong, I love her. She's been my best friend for as long as I can remember, but she's only ever had one girlfriend. The breakup devastated her. The reasons leading up to it, and the actual reason for it in the end."

"I know," Maddie said with a nod. She really didn't know, but she hoped Kelly hadn't made the story up just to catch them in their lie. "She told me all about it."

"I doubt that," Kelly said with a snort, and Maddie just smiled at her. "She doesn't talk about it with anyone. I just want to make sure you know I have her back. If you hurt her, you'll have to deal with me."

Maddie stared at her back as Kelly turned and walked away. What the hell? She hadn't expected that. She felt her heart swell at the realization Kelly felt so fiercely protective of Savannah.

No, she told herself, your heart shouldn't be swelling with anything concerning Savannah. This was nothing but a ruse, and she'd do well to remember it. But it was so damn easy to fall into Savannah's blue-gray eyes. She had a way of making Maddie feel like she was the only person who mattered when they were together.

She glanced up and saw Savannah looking at her, a worried expression on her face. Maddie had never mastered the art of reading lips, but she knew when Savannah mouthed *are you okay?* She forced a smile and nodded with a wave to let her know everything was fine.

But was it? After being pulled in to Savannah's orbit, she wasn't sure anything was ever going to be fine again.

Chapter Seventeen

Savannah took her seat next to Court after giving her speech at the reception, and her heart was beating way too fast. The people in attendance had laughed in all the right places, and Lana didn't seem too put out about the references to Court's somewhat colored past.

She'd been acutely aware of Maddie's camera focusing on her for part of the speech, and it had unnerved her a little bit. What did the lens reveal to her? Did she see the easygoing woman she tried to portray, or did it reveal the insecurities she felt deep down in her soul? The self-doubt she'd harbored since college.

The feeling of never being enough for someone else. It was something she'd never spoken to anyone about. Not Lisa or Faith, not Noah, not even Kelly. None of them knew the dark places she'd gone to when Shauna crushed her world ten years ago.

"You did good, Wells," Court said with a hand on her shoulder, effectively pulling her back out of her own head. Savannah smiled.

"Yeah? I didn't send you down the road to divorce?"

"Hardly." Court laughed. "Lana already knew about everything you mentioned."

"Wow," Savannah said. She dug her nails into her palms to distract herself from the tears she felt threatening to fall. What the hell was it about weddings? "I'm really happy you found each other, Court. You deserve to be happy."

"So do you," Court replied, glancing over toward the camera and smiling. When she looked back at her, Savannah thought Court understood more than she ever let on. "Promise me you'll think about the things I said earlier. Don't dismiss Maddie without really giving her an opportunity to show you how great she is."

Savannah watched Maddie as Court spoke, but she turned and met Court's eyes with a nod.

"I promise I'll think about it," she said. "I can't promise any more than that though."

"Hey, it's a start. You know you can call me if you ever need to talk, right? Just not in the next two weeks. I'll be a little busy with the honeymoon and all." Court winked and squeezed her shoulder before letting go and turning her attention to her new wife.

People were going in and out of the house to get food from the buffet Lana's mother had prepared for the wedding. It wasn't anything fancy because Lana and Court made sure she didn't go all out. It looked as though most of the guests were opting for the lasagna, and Savannah realized she was hungrier than she'd thought she was.

While she was waiting in the line for food, she felt someone behind her bump into her. She turned and saw Maddie smiling at her, and she couldn't help but smile back. She had a way of making Savannah believe anything was possible, and she had a feeling it would only lead to heartbreak.

"What was Kelly talking to you about?" Savannah asked, remembering the look on her face as Kelly walked away from her before the ceremony. "You looked a little upset. Was she hitting on you?"

"She was warning me," Maddie said with a shrug indicating it was no big deal.

"About what?" Savannah looked around for Kelly, wanting to give a warning of her own.

"She said you've been hurt in the past, and if I hurt you, I'd have to answer to her." Maddie held her eyes, and Savannah was uncomfortable with the pity she saw there. "I think it was sweet of her to stand up for you."

"Sweet?" Savannah asked, feeling anything but grateful for Kelly's interference. "She had no right to tell you anything about my past."

"Hey, she was just looking out for her friend," Maddie said as she grabbed her hand. "And I would hope, in spite of the fact we're fake dating, that you think of me as a friend as well."

Savannah looked down at her feet for a moment, feeling a little off kilter. Of course she thought of Maddie as a friend. The problem was, she was beginning to think of her as more than just a friend. She slid her fingers between Maddie's and squeezed gently. "I'm sorry," she said. "Of course you're a friend."

"It's okay," Maddie said, but her expression told Savannah otherwise. "A bit of a warning for you though…I think she was trying to trip me up. She was digging to see if we really are dating. I'm pretty sure she didn't believe me when I said you'd already told me about it."

Savannah felt a bit lost when Maddie released her hand, and the distance between them tore at her heartstrings. She wanted to be closer to Maddie, but she didn't know how to go about it. She'd spent so long keeping women at a distance, she wasn't even sure she could vocalize what she wanted.

Savannah asked Maddie to come in when they returned from the wedding, and she agreed to, but needed to go home and let Duke out first. They'd been gone for hours, and she didn't want the dog peeing in the house.

While she waited, Savannah got out of her tux and into a more relaxed pair of shorts and a well-worn Kingsville Warriors T-shirt. She paced in front of the couch, wondering if she was doing the right thing. She'd decided to tell Maddie about Shauna.

She wasn't sure how much Kelly had let slip, but it had to have been Shauna she was referencing when she'd talked to Maddie. She'd tried to corner Kelly more than once at the reception to question her about it, but Kelly managed to skirt the issue every time. Leo stared at her with typical feline disinterest, and she couldn't help but chuckle at his bored look.

"I wish I could be as aloof as you are, little man," she said with a quick scratch under his chin just as there was a knock at the door. She closed her eyes and took a deep breath before going to answer it. She moved aside as she pulled the door open so Maddie could enter. "Hi."

"Hi," Maddie said as she walked past. She looked Savannah up and down, then let out a breath and shook her head. "As much as I liked you in the tux, I have to say, you look even better like this."

Even though the words made Savannah uncomfortable, the way Maddie was looking at her caused her pulse to quicken, and a thrum began low in her belly. She walked to the kitchen so Maddie wouldn't see the desire she was sure was in her eyes. She grabbed a couple of water bottles from the fridge and slowly made her way back to where Maddie was sitting on the couch.

"What exactly did Kelly say to you?"

"She said you were devastated by a girl in college." Maddie took the water she offered but set it on the end table without opening it. "I didn't want her to think we didn't talk about things, so I said you'd already told me."

"And she knew better," Savannah said with a laugh. She shook her head when Maddie nodded in response. "She knows I don't tell anyone about it. But I want to tell you."

"You don't have to, Savannah."

"I know," she said with a nod. "I really do want to. And besides, if she questions you again about it, I want to make sure you really do know what happened."

"Is this the reason you're *perpetually* single?"

Savannah nodded and ran her fingers through her hair. She leaned forward, her forearms resting on her thighs just above the knees, and she rubbed her hands together. Where did she even begin?

"There was this girl, Shauna," she said after a moment, deciding the beginning was the best place. "We met in our sophomore year. She pursued me, and I resisted. For almost an entire year. She was rather persistent though and I finally gave in. Everything was great for a while. By the time my senior year was underway, I was so busy between my classes, hockey, and trying to get accepted into vet school, but she said she understood."

Savannah paused for a moment, trying to tamp down all the feelings she felt resurfacing. Feelings of betrayal, hurt, and an immense sensation of inadequacy. Shauna had spent months convincing her she loved her and would always be at her side, and Savannah had stupidly believed her.

Maddie was watching her closely, but was thankfully quiet to give Savannah the time she needed to tell this story. Leo was on Maddie's lap enjoying the belly rub she was giving him and purring loudly.

"Turned out she didn't *really* understand, because she began looking elsewhere for the companionship I couldn't give her. Three weeks before graduation I came home after my last exam of the year, and she was just carrying out the last box of her things." Savannah shook her head and leaned back on the couch, looking up at the ceiling. "She accused me of being more in love with becoming a veterinarian than her. And her new boyfriend agreed. Although he seemed to be really happy about the situation."

"So, she was bi?" Maddie asked carefully. "Did you know?"

"I assumed she was a lesbian," Savannah said with a shake of her head. "Shame on me for not asking. Honestly? I think she was a straight girl who wanted to have fun experimenting with a dyke before settling down. She married the guy and they have two kids now."

"I'm so sorry that happened to you, Savannah," Maddie said quietly. Savannah looked at her and could see she was sincere in her words, but it didn't really make her feel any better.

"Since getting my DVM license, nothing much has changed. I'm still busy most of the time and have little to offer a woman as far as a relationship goes." Savannah took a drink of her water and chuckled humorlessly. "I still spend a lot of time on hockey during the season, and a lot of time at the vet's office the rest of the time. It's easier being single."

"Don't you get lonely?" Maddie asked. "I'm not talking about sex, I know there's plenty of opportunity out there for that, but for companionship. For someone to talk to about your day, about your dreams."

"I have Kelly for that," Savannah said with a dismissive wave. "I don't need to worry about a woman at home who might be feeling neglected and looking for something better."

"I'm not going to try to tell you you're wrong," Maddie said as she reached over and took Savannah's hand. "You have valid reasons for feeling the way you do. But you have to know not all women are like that, right?"

On some level she did know it, but it seemed like too much work to try and find a woman who wasn't. Maybe Maddie could be that woman, but how could she know for sure? Only time would tell, and she wasn't sure she wanted to put the time into finding out just to be hurt again.

CHAPTER EIGHTEEN

The next couple of months went by quickly for Savannah. She and Maddie spent a lot of time together going to family functions and spending time with friends. They never talked again about relationships. It seemed they'd fallen into a routine of spending most evenings together, and as a result they were becoming closer. They held hands a lot, but they'd only kissed once or twice, and it always seemed to be Savannah who would put the brakes on. She was quite sure Maddie would have been happy to let things progress further, but Savannah couldn't let it. She was already too close to falling for her, and that would only end badly.

"Let's go for an undefeated season, ladies," Gail said with a grin a few minutes before they were going to take the ice for the beginning of their first game of the season. Gail said it at the start of every season, but every player knew it was all but impossible to do it. It was a nice dream though, at least until they suffered their first loss.

"Going to introduce us to your new girlfriend, Wells?" Jen Hilton asked as she elbowed her in the back while walking past her.

"Everyone's already met her, Hilton," Kelly said with a wink for Savannah. "Well, everyone who matters anyway."

A few people laughed, and Savannah held back a smile at the way Hilton's cheeks turned red. She was obviously pissed, and Savannah would no doubt have to deal with her at some point, but since Court was traded, Hilton had pretty much kept to herself. She knew people blamed her for their captain being traded, but a couple of years gone from it, she was beginning to be a little more vocal again. Maybe she thought enough time had passed and they'd gotten over the way things went down. It was Hilton's blatant homophobia that had gotten her into trouble before, so Savannah wasn't surprised the first thing out of her mouth was some snide comment about her girlfriend.

"Everyone who was at Court's wedding met her," Savannah said. She stood and grabbed her helmet before pointedly looking in Hilton's direction. "They're the people who matter."

"I would never go to a *fake* wedding," Hilton shot back as she took a couple of steps toward her. Savannah stood her ground and was well aware of all the eyes on them. She was named captain of the team after Court left, and this interaction would no doubt serve to set the tone for the entire season.

"I'm not nearly as laid-back as Court was, Hilton," Savannah said, her tone even. She didn't want an altercation, but she needed to let her know she wasn't going to back down if Hilton insisted on riding her the way she did Court. "So you might want to keep your bigoted opinions to yourself."

Savannah secured her helmet as everyone waited for the response, but Hilton obviously knew she was outnumbered. Court and Lana had sent a group invitation to the entire team for their wedding, and Jen Hilton was the only one who hadn't attended. As far as Savannah was concerned, that alone should have let her know she was the lone minority in the locker room.

"Whatever," Hilton muttered as she walked away from her. Savannah let out a relieved breath and grabbed her gloves.

"Wells," Gail said from her office door. "A quick word?"

"I won't let her push me this year, Coach," Savannah said after closing the door behind her.

"And I wouldn't expect you to," Gail said. "I only wanted to thank you for the way you handled the situation. I just want to make sure nothing turns physical."

"It won't, as long as she doesn't start anything."

"I guess I can't ask for anything more." Gail nodded and motioned for her to head back out and join the team, who were heading out to the ice.

Savannah hit the ice to cheers from the crowd. She raised her stick in the air in acknowledgment as she rounded the ice behind the Warriors net. Kelly caught up to her and gave her a playful nudge with her shoulder.

"There's nothing like the love from the fans on opening night, is there?" she asked.

"Certainly gets the blood pumping." Savannah knew she was grinning from ear to ear, as was Kelly. The roar of the crowd always had the same effect. The adrenaline started flowing, and they all felt invincible. "I love this."

Savannah, Kelly, Alex, and two defensive players stayed at center ice when the rest of the team headed to the bench since they were starting the game. Savannah closed her eyes and took in a deep breath as the national anthem started, and she felt her heart racing. Damn, this feeling was amazing. It never grew old in her eyes. When the anthem was over, the crowd began cheering again, and the starting five skaters swarmed the goalie, Charlotte Greene. They all whacked her pads with their sticks in a good luck gesture, and then they headed to center ice for the opening face-off.

Alex pointed with her stick to show Savannah where she wanted her positioned for the face-off, and with another deep breath, Savannah readied herself. When the puck was dropped, the crowd noise disappeared in Savannah's consciousness, and nothing else existed for her but what was happening on the ice.

The puck went to Kelly, and they headed up the ice. She passed across the ice to Savannah, who saw Alex had gotten out ahead of the defender, so she sent a quick pass to her and Alex flipped it over the goalie's shoulder for the first goal of the season.

They ended up behind 2-1 after the first period, thanks to Jen Hilton coughing up the puck in their own zone leading to both the goals.

"We're better than this, ladies," Savannah said as she stood in the center of the locker room. Everyone was sitting so they were facing her. She looked everyone in the eye as she spoke. "This first period will not define the rest of the season. Pick it up. Turnovers in our own zone are not acceptable. Understood?"

"Why not direct your comments to the one who needs to hear it?"

Savannah swung her gaze toward Nancy Myer, a winger on Hilton's line, who had made the comment as she was looking right at Hilton.

"Because everyone needs to hear it. No one is above making a mistake or two, and when it happens, it happens to the entire team, not to just one player." Savannah looked away from Myer when she was sure her point had made its desired impact. She purposely resisted looking at Hilton because she was sure she would be angry as hell.

"What the hell, Van?" Kelly asked when she took a seat next to her in front of her locker. "Why not call Hilton out by name? It wasn't anybody's fault but hers."

"I'm wearing the C on my jersey, Kelly." Savannah ran a hand through her sweat soaked hair before tightening the laces on her skates. God knew she wanted nothing more than to call Hilton out, but she had a job to do. They all did. Unfortunately, it fell on her to make sure they all did what they were supposed to. "She knows what she did wrong. You just need to worry about what you're supposed to do, and she'll either fix it, or she won't. Either way, it has nothing to do with you."

"Whatever," Kelly muttered.

"Maybe she'll keep making the same mistakes and end up playing her way right out of Kingsville."

She could only hope.

❖

Maddie didn't know all the ins and outs of hockey, but she was pretty sure Jen Hilton was not a good player. Not if the first period was any indication. But, it was only the first game of the year, so maybe they were all just trying to find their rhythm again. Of course, Savannah's line clicked right away, so that excuse didn't seem to hold much water.

Thanks to the time she'd spent with Savannah during the off-season, Maddie knew more about the game than she had before. At least she could follow conversations about it now, and not sound like such a newbie when she did decide to comment on something.

She looked at the pictures she'd taken from the pregame warm-ups, and was going over the shots from the first period when she felt a hand touch her elbow. She looked up to find Dana standing next to her.

"Ooh, I like that one," Dana said, indicating the photo she had on the screen. It was Savannah just after she passed the puck to Alex Winter for their only goal thus far.

"It is a nice one, isn't it?" Savannah smiled as she looked at it again. The look of determination on Savannah's face was sexy as hell. She'd looked up to find Savannah just as she snapped the picture, and it appeared as though she was looking right at her. It caused a flutter in her chest.

"In all honesty, I'm pretty sure she'd be physically unable to take a bad picture," Dana said with a shoulder bump and a grin.

"Seriously?" Maddie laughed. "Does your husband know you're here drooling over my girlfriend?"

"It's his own damn fault for having to work late so I had to bring Amy here on my own tonight." Dana shrugged and they both laughed, because Trent knew he had nothing to worry about. Dana was so in love with him it made Maddie envious. She so wanted to have someone love her the way Dana loved her husband.

"I have to head over toward the locker room, because I need to get some shots from that end of the ice during the next period." Maddie began putting things in her camera bag as she spoke.

"You want to come for dinner this weekend?" Dana asked.

"It would have to be Friday, because they play again Saturday, so I need to be here to take pictures."

"What are they using all these photos for?"

"They're for all kinds of things. Game day programs, calendars, some will go to the newspaper, and they'll be selling prints at the souvenir shops."

"Cool. And do they just pay you a flat fee for everything, or do you make money on prints and calendars?"

"My commission is based on the amount they bring in for everything." Maddie shrugged. This job had the potential to be very lucrative for her, and it certainly didn't hurt that she could look at Savannah while she was working.

Chapter Nineteen

They were one month into the season, and the Warriors had lost only two games. Savannah was leading the team in points, and there was harmony on the team. Sort of. Jen Hilton was still making her snide comments whenever she had the opportunity, but Savannah was refusing to let her get under her skin. Hilton had been in her share of scraps, mostly because she couldn't keep her mouth shut on the ice. Players on the opposing teams generally dropped their gloves with her when she'd push someone too far. Savannah wished she could do the same thing sometimes.

"Thanksgiving is only a couple of weeks away," Maddie said one night.

They'd taken to spending an hour or two together after games, usually at Maddie's house, but tonight they were at Savannah's. Kelly wasn't very happy about it, because they used to go out dancing after games in the past. Savannah had missed it at first, but the more time she spent with Maddie, the more time she *wanted* to spend with her. It wasn't a concept she really understood, especially concerning a woman she hadn't ever slept with.

"Yeah," Savannah said with a nod. "It's crazy how fast time flies. It seems like just yesterday it was the Fourth of July."

"We haven't really talked about what we're going to do," Maddie said, sounding tentative. "I'm assuming Lisa and Faith are expecting me to be there with you."

"I hadn't really given it much thought, but I guess it would be a little strange if you didn't show up with me," Savannah said. "What about your family? Do you usually go to your parents'?"

"Usually, yes, but they're actually coming here to Dana's this year." Maddie's lips lifted in a smile, but Savannah didn't think it was because she was happy. It actually looked more like a grimace. "I know they'll be expecting to meet you, but I don't know if I really want to subject you to that."

"Are they really so terrible?" Savannah chuckled, but then turned serious as she considered the other option. "Or am I that terrible?"

"Not you," Maddie said as she shook her head. She reached over and placed her hand over Savannah's, squeezing gently. "My mother is a bit overbearing, and my father thinks no one is good enough for me, no matter who they are, or what they do for a living."

"I see. And you're saying he wouldn't be swayed by the fact I'm a semipro female hockey player who doesn't make enough money to support myself, let alone someone else?"

"Yeah, not so much, but to be fair, it wouldn't sway him to learn you're a veterinarian either. He's an equal opportunity girlfriend hater."

"Good to know, I guess," Savannah said with a sigh. Based on the glowing description of her parents, Savannah wasn't sure she ever wanted to meet them. "You could always go to Dana's on your own. Tell them my moms needed me for something."

"It might work," Maddie said thoughtfully. Her hand was still on Savannah's, and neither of them made a move to change it.

Savannah stared at their hands on the couch between them and turned her hand over to entwine their fingers. She was beginning to feel too much for Maddie, but she didn't know how to stop it without putting an end to their fake relationship. And for some reason, she didn't want to end it. She enjoyed the time they spent together. She liked the idea of Maddie accompanying her to Thanksgiving dinner as her girlfriend.

"Do you miss going out to the bars?" Maddie asked after the silence must have become too much. "Because I know Kelly keeps asking you to go. You can, you know."

"Honestly, I did in the beginning, but I don't really care now," Savannah said, surprising herself at the answer. It was true though. Yes, much to her dismay, Lisa had been right. She wasn't going to find anyone who mattered in the bar. And like it or not, Maddie was someone who mattered. "I really like just hanging out with you."

"Really?" Maddie was obviously skeptical, if her expression was any indication. Her nose was crinkled, and her brow furrowed. "Because if you're anything like Kelly, I'm sure you go there with one thing in mind, and it ain't happening between us."

Savannah laughed and shook her head. "No, it's not." She'd told Maddie about her rule of not getting involved with neighbors, and she seemed to understand it. There were times though Savannah was sure they were both willing to abandon that rule.

"Just know it's okay with your fake girlfriend if you want to go out and have a little fun, okay?"

"Or my fake girlfriend could go out with us," Savannah suggested.

She watched as Maddie's eyes darted around the room, looking everywhere but at her. It was obvious the idea of going out with her and Kelly made her uncomfortable. She probably thought she would pick someone up and go home with them, leaving Maddie stranded. For one thing, she couldn't very well do it in front of Kelly since she thought they were really dating, and for another, she would never do that to Maddie.

"Maybe," Maddie said, not sounding too enthusiastic at the suggestion.

"How about this weekend?" Savannah asked before she could think too much about making the suggestion. "We have a game Saturday night. Kelly will want to go out dancing after. Will you come with us if she asks me to go?"

Maddie seemed to consider it for a moment before finally nodding her head. "Yeah, I think I might like that."

"Cool."

She pulled her hand away from Savannah and got to her feet. "And on that note, I think I should get home and take care of my dog."

Savannah walked her to the door and they stood there a little awkwardly. Maddie hadn't kissed her in quite some time, and Savannah knew she was leaving it up to her if it was ever going to happen again. After a few moments, Maddie smiled and reached for the doorknob.

"I'll see you soon," she said quietly before walking out and heading back to her house.

Savannah fought with herself to not call out to her, to ask her to come back. She shut the door to quell any temptation to do exactly that. She leaned her back against the door and saw Leo looking at her as though she'd lost her mind. She had to laugh, because he might have been right.

Maddie let Duke out into the yard and poured herself a glass of wine while she waited for him to finish his business. Once he was back inside, she sat on the couch with him by her side, his head in her lap. She scratched behind his ears and smiled when he groaned in satisfaction.

She thought back on her conversation with Savannah a few short minutes earlier. She chuckled. She really didn't want to go to a lesbian bar with her and Kelly. The last thing she needed was to witness Savannah with another woman. God, she was in over her head.

It was becoming glaringly obvious she was going to have to make the first move if anything was ever going to happen between the two of them. She knew Savannah was feeling the same pull she was. It was written all over her face when she looked at Maddie. And Maddie doubted Savannah had any idea how much her eyes revealed her desire.

"Christ," she said to the empty room. Duke lifted his head and looked at her. He was used to her talking to herself, but he always held out hope she was talking to him, and he might get a treat out of it. When he finally decided he wasn't getting anything, he settled in again with a loud sigh. "How would she react if I did make a move on her?"

It was an interesting thought, and one she might revisit somewhere down the road. She chuckled again when she thought about her parents meeting Savannah at Thanksgiving.

She loved her parents, but her mother was incessantly quizzing anyone she brought home to meet them. It was as though she needed to find out absolutely everything about someone in the short time she was in their presence.

Her father on the other hand, was simply convinced no one was good enough for his little girl. For some reason he hadn't been the same way with Dana, and he always said it was because Madison was his baby, and nobody was going to take advantage of his baby as long as he had any fight left in him.

She loved him for that, but God, it could be so annoying. She knew she shouldn't be thinking about a long-term relationship with Savannah, but she couldn't help it. It was so easy to picture them together in the future. Because of that, she really didn't want to subject her to her parents this early on. Maddie knew without a doubt they would scare her away before she had the chance to see where this was all going to lead.

CHAPTER TWENTY

"Call me crazy, but it sounds like you might be falling in love," Court said. Savannah had called her the next morning to find out if she was out of her mind for inviting Maddie to go out dancing with her and Kelly.

Savannah laughed out loud at the comment, but it was forced. She'd been struggling with the possibility she was actually falling for Maddie, but had convinced herself it was only because of the close proximity they had.

Seriously, when you were fake dating, did you really have to spend so much time alone together? Who exactly were they trying to convince when ninety-five percent of the time they spent together was just the two of them?

Comparatively, they'd spent very little time with family as a "couple." Maddie insisted she not go with her for Thanksgiving dinner, and while Savannah's initial response was to be relieved, she realized later it had actually bruised her ego. Was she not good enough? Or just not important enough to warrant meeting the parents? Either way, it hurt.

"You are definitely crazy, Court." Savannah glanced at the clock and saw she still had a few minutes to talk before she had to leave for practice.

"You don't sound very convincing."

"I don't need to," Savannah said. "There is no way I'm falling in love with her, or anyone else for that matter."

"Have you slept with her?" Court lowered her voice, probably because she didn't want Lana to hear what she was saying. Or maybe she just did it to be dramatic. Savannah wouldn't put it past her.

"No."

"But you want to, right?"

"No." She answered too quickly, and sounded more emphatic than she felt. She heard Court chuckle and thought she heard a whispered *yeah, right.* "Fine. Maybe I do, but it won't happen. She lives next door. What happens when she inevitably realizes she needs more from me than I can give? I won't quit playing hockey, and when I'm not doing something related to that, I'm working at the vet's office. I don't have the time to give to a relationship."

"You are so full of shit," Court said with a sigh. Because Court seemed to be calling her on a weekly basis and didn't understand her hesitancy at getting involved with anyone, Savannah had finally told her all about Shauna and what happened at college. Savannah was beginning to regret telling her. "I get that the ghost of relationships past is whispering in your ear, telling you you aren't good enough, but you've got to ignore it. Maddie isn't Shauna. Not everyone is going to demand as much from you as she did. If Maddie's worth it, then you make compromises. You find the time to give to her."

"Listen to Court, Savannah," came Lana's voice through the line. It sounded as though she was on the other side of the room from Court. "She has experience in that area."

"Did you hear?" Court chuckled, and Savannah joined in.

"I did," she replied.

"Is Maddie worth it?"

"I don't know." Savannah was quickly coming to the decision Maddie was worth it, but she wasn't about to admit it to Court.

"But you think she might be, am I right?"

"I really don't know, Court."

"Did you buy her a Christmas present?"

"Yeah," Savannah admitted with a sigh. She looked at the box she had on the coffee table that contained a gold chain. Maddie didn't wear much jewelry, but she'd mentioned she had a gold necklace she lost at some point between leaving Chicago and moving into the house next door. She hadn't even given it much thought; she just knew she wanted to get her something Savannah hoped would make her happy. Let her know she was actually listening when Maddie talked. "A necklace."

"Good." Court was grinning, Savannah was sure she heard it in her tone of voice. "If you feel something for her, you need to let her know. That's all I'm saying. Let go of the past, Van. Live for the future."

They talked for a few more minutes before she finally told Court she needed to get to practice. After disconnecting the call, Savannah sat there in silence, a million different things racing through her mind. She did feel something for Maddie. There was no point in lying to herself about it. And maybe Court was right. Maybe it *was* time to let Maddie know.

"Jesus, Van," Kelly said as they were in the locker room changing after their practice. "You never go to the bars anymore. This woman has you whipped. I just hope the sex is worth it."

Savannah turned her head and bit her bottom lip to keep from laughing. How would Kelly react if she were to tell her they hadn't had sex? She was tempted to find out but knew she'd never tell her the truth.

"It is, trust me," Savannah finally said.

"Aren't you tired of being tied to one woman yet?"

Savannah knew this was why Kelly didn't give her a hard time in the beginning. She was certain it would never last. It pissed Savannah off to realize the truth of it, but she really couldn't blame her. In all the time they'd known each other, Shauna was the only woman she'd been with more than once or twice.

"No, Kelly, I'm not."

"Huh. I've got to hand it to you, Van, I only gave it six weeks," Kelly said with a shrug. "And here you are about to hit six months. I'm impressed, but I still think you need to come out with me sometime. Bring the little lady if you want."

"Actually, we talked about going out with you tomorrow night after the game."

"No shit?" Kelly was beaming. "Awesome."

"You're crazy," Savannah said, shaking her head, but unable to stop grinning at Kelly's exuberance.

"Maybe I am, but do you want to know what I think?" Kelly was tying her shoes but glanced at Savannah.

"Not really, but I have feeling you're going to tell me anyway."

"Damn right." Kelly finished what she was doing and sat up straight before glancing around the locker room. She leaned closer to Savannah and lowered her voice. "I don't think you've slept with her at all."

"What?" Savannah tried to sound indignant, but wasn't sure she was actually pulling it off. "Like you said, we're going on six months here, Kelly. You know me better than that. You honestly think I'd go for so long without getting her into bed?"

"All I know is what I see." Kelly shrugged. She stood and grabbed her equipment bag but then leaned down again. "She looks at you like you're a porterhouse steak, and she hasn't eaten in months."

She wanted to argue. She wanted to tell Kelly she was delusional. The only problem was Kelly was right. Savannah had tried to ignore the way Maddie looked at her, and the desire in her eyes. Kelly nodded and chuckled.

"You probably aren't even dating her, are you?"

"You're nuts," Savannah said. She stood and picked up her own equipment bag before heading for the door. "If what you're suggesting is true, then why haven't I gone to the bars with you for the past six months?"

"I haven't figured that part out yet, but I will," Kelly called after her as Savannah left the locker room.

Damn it, Savannah thought, shaking her head. It was time to let Maddie know how she felt. If everything worked out, great. If not, then they'd have to end their fake relationship. It was probably about time to do it regardless, because it was getting more and more difficult every day to separate what was real and what wasn't.

FACE OFF

CHAPTER TWENTY-ONE

"Why do you seem so nervous?" Maddie asked Savannah after they'd parked the car and were walking toward the club. Every time the door to the place opened, the bass to the music could be heard. It excited Maddie. She was actually going out dancing with Savannah. Sure, they'd danced at Court and Lana's wedding, but this was different somehow.

"Do I?" Savannah asked, glancing at her. She stopped walking a few feet from the door, and Maddie turned to face her. "I guess I am. Kelly doesn't think we've ever slept together."

Maddie wasn't sure what to say, so she just stared at her for a moment. She thought they'd been pretty convincing about their relationship. Everyone else seemed to believe it, but why was Kelly still unconvinced?

"Who knew we'd actually have to sleep together for Kelly to believe we're dating?" she said, hoping to alleviate the awkwardness that seemed to have settled over them. It had the desired effect, if Savannah's laughter was anything to go by. She took Savannah's hand and started walking toward the entrance again, hoping she was exhibiting more confidence then she actually felt. "We'll just have to be more affectionate then, right?"

"Right." Savannah nodded, but Maddie didn't think she sounded too keen on the idea.

· 149 ·

"Just hold my hand a lot, kiss my cheek a few times, and dance with me. A lot." Maddie smiled at her and nodded, and Savannah eventually nodded back and seemed to be getting more comfortable with her role for the evening. Obviously, she was okay with Maddie taking the lead. "By the time the night is over, she'll have no doubt we're sleeping together."

"Hey, Savannah," a woman in a skintight dress said as she pressed against her after they'd paid their cover and were headed to the bar. "Haven't seen you in a while."

"That's because I have a girlfriend now," Savannah said as she held their hands up to show the woman. Maddie's heart swelled.

"Oh," the woman said, looking equal parts devastated and angry. "You said you never wanted a girlfriend."

"I didn't, until I met Maddie." Savannah looked at her and smiled before leaning in and giving her a kiss on the lips. It was chaste, but it still managed to send Maddie's pulse skyrocketing, and she couldn't help but smile back at her. "She's everything I didn't know I wanted."

"I'm happy for you," the woman said, sounding anything but as she turned and walked away.

"Who was she?" Maddie asked.

"I don't even remember her name," Savannah said with a shrug. They continued their trek to the bar and found Kelly sitting alone.

"About time you two showed up." Kelly turned on her barstool to look at them. She glanced at their hands and smirked before glancing at Maddie's face. "I was beginning to think you changed your mind about coming tonight."

"Actually, I did, but Maddie insisted we come," Savannah said after ordering a round for the three of them.

"Yeah, she wanted to stay home," Maddie said, going with it. She bumped Savannah with her hip. "She wanted to keep me all to herself."

Savannah grinned and put her arms around her waist, pulling her close and kissing her again. It was less chaste this time, but it didn't last long enough in Maddie's opinion. It was just as well though, because Kelly was watching them with a little too much interest.

"You guys are sickening," Kelly said, but she was laughing. She clapped Savannah on the back. "I think it's great."

A couple more women came to try to chat up Savannah, but she always put them off by putting an arm around Maddie's waist. In fact she hadn't let go of her after the last woman walked away. Maddie leaned close to her and raised her voice in order to be heard above the music.

"Come dance with me," she said. Savannah set her drink down on the bar and allowed her to lead her onto the dance floor. They danced to a couple of songs before it switched to a slow one, and Maddie started to head back to the bar.

"Where are you going?" Savannah asked, grabbing her hand and pulling her back. Her arms went around Maddie's waist, and their lips were only a few inches apart. Their bodies were even closer. Maddie swallowed hard as they stared into each other's eyes.

"You don't have to do this," she said.

"I want to," Savannah replied. Her hands moved to Maddie's hips as they swayed to the music. Maddie's arms went around Savannah's neck and she pulled her closer until their foreheads were touching.

"You are so incredibly sexy," Maddie said, unable to help herself. She was tired of holding back her feelings. Her heart was thudding against her ribcage as she waited for Savannah to say something in response.

"Yeah?" Savannah gave her a lopsided grin and her head tilted slightly. "And you're the most beautiful woman in this place."

"You're sweet," Maddie said with a chuckle. She shook her head. "I'm definitely not your type if these women are anything to go by."

"What do you mean?"

"Look around, Savannah," she said, and Savannah did just that. "I don't wear makeup, I don't dress all girly. You're obviously attracted to more feminine women."

Savannah nodded slowly before meeting her eyes again. They danced in silence for a few moments before Savannah pressed her cheek against Maddie's so she could speak directly into her ear.

"I'll admit I used to be attracted to that kind of woman," she said before sucking in Maddie's earlobe. "But now? It's absolutely you I'm attracted to. You don't need makeup. And you're beautiful no matter what you're wearing."

Savannah sighed when Maddie's arms tightened around her neck. Her hands moved down Maddie's hips and around to cup her backside. Maddie groaned in her ear, and Savannah felt the wetness between her own legs. She wasn't exactly sure when she'd made the decision to not hold back her feelings anymore, but if Maddie pressed this tightly against her was the result, she was sorry she'd waited so long.

"There's no one around to hear us, so you don't have to pretend," Maddie said breathlessly.

"I'm not pretending," Savannah said. Maddie stopped swaying to the music and took a step back to look in her eyes. Savannah smiled and nodded at the question in Maddie's eyes. "I'm completely serious, Maddie. When I told that woman you were everything I thought I never wanted? I meant it. God help me, I never meant anything more in my life."

"Really?" Maddie asked. "You aren't just messing with me?"

"No, I'm not." Savannah leaned in and kissed her. She parted her lips when Maddie's tongue demanded entry and felt as though her knees were going to give out. The throbbing between her legs was instant when Maddie's tongue slid slowly against her own. Savannah moved her hands up Maddie's sides and touched her breast, which caused Maddie to step back again. They were both breathing hard as Maddie searched her eyes. She evidently found what she was looking for because she grabbed Savannah's hand and began leading her off the dance floor.

"Let's go home," she said.

Savannah smiled and allowed her to lead her back over to where Kelly was now talking with a woman who'd taken the bar stool next to her.

"Hey, Kel," Savannah said as she placed a hand on her shoulder. "We're going to head out."

"You just got here," Kelly said, turning to look at her. She glanced between them and smiled with a nod. "Yeah, you should go before you rip each other's clothes off right here in front of everyone. I'll catch you later."

Savannah cursed the long ride home as they got into the car. Maybe they should get a hotel room. No, that seemed cheap and sleazy. If she was going to make love with Maddie, it should be in one of their own beds.

CHAPTER TWENTY-TWO

The closer they got to their neighborhood, the more nervous Savannah was getting. They were really going to do this. She was elated, but at the same time apprehensive about it. What would it mean for them going forward?

"Your place or mine?" Maddie asked. Savannah noticed the blush on her cheeks and thought it was sweet. Obviously, she wasn't the only one who was feeling anxious.

"Yours," Savannah said but then looked over at her house. "I want to go check on Leo really quick though, all right? Give me five minutes?"

"Okay."

Savannah didn't really need to check on Leo. He was completely fine by himself even if he did occasionally get his nose out of joint when she'd be gone for hours on end. She just needed a few minutes to calm herself and wrap her head around what was happening.

For just a second she considered going to her own bed and not going back to Maddie's. But only for a second. There was no doubt in her mind she wanted this. She made sure Leo had food and fresh water then took a deep breath and headed next door.

Maddie opened the door with her hand grasping Duke's collar. He was panting and wagging his tail as he looked up at Savannah.

"He's happy to see you," Maddie said with a smile.

"Is that right?" Savannah walked in and crouched down so she was on his level. She scratched behind his ears and Maddie closed the door before letting go of him. "I'm glad to see you too, boy."

He licked her face a few times, causing her to laugh, then she stood and faced Maddie. She noticed there was soft music playing, and she saw a couple glasses of wine on the coffee table over Maddie's shoulder.

"I'm glad to see you, too," she said, stepping closer and attempting to kiss her. She looked irresistible in the tank top and shorts she'd changed into. Maddie put a hand on the center of her chest and shook her head.

"You aren't kissing me after Duke just had his tongue all over your face. There's no telling where his mouth has been." Maddie made a "yuck" face and shook her head. "You know where the bathroom is. Go wash your face and I'll be waiting in the living room."

Savannah scrubbed her face and then stood there looking at herself in the mirror above the sink. She nodded once, affirming to herself she did want this. The problem was, she didn't want it to be just one night. She was definitely falling for Maddie in a big way, but what if Maddie didn't want the same things she did from this relationship? She stood up straight and took in a deep breath.

She heard Maddie talking to Duke as she approached the living room from the hallway. When she rounded the corner, Duke ran right to her, then skidded to a stop in front of her and plopped his butt down, his tail going a mile a minute. She scratched his ears as he walked along beside her to the couch.

"So what did Kelly say was her reason for not believing we're sleeping together?" Maddie asked as soon as Savannah made herself comfortable.

"Apparently, what gave it away is the way you look at me." Savannah said, concentrating on Duke, who was resting his chin on her thigh so she could continue scratching his ears.

"How exactly do I look at you?"

"According to her, and I'm quoting here," Savannah said as she looked up at her. "Like I'm a porterhouse steak, and you haven't eaten in months."

Maddie laughed out loud, causing Savannah to chuckle as well. Maddie sat there with her hand over her mouth and shook her head.

"Have you ever thought I was looking at you like that?"

Savannah shrugged. Of course she did, but she wasn't sure she could admit it. Maddie was just looking at her, one eyebrow arched in question. She obviously wasn't going to let it go without an actual answer.

"Maybe. A time or two."

"Should I apologize?" Maddie didn't look like she was going to apologize for anything. In fact, she was looking at her like that now. She shrugged and grinned. "Pizza may be my favorite food, but I can certainly admit I enjoy a good steak now and again."

Savannah swallowed hard when Maddie moved so she was only a few inches away from her on the couch. Her pulse quickened and she ached with the desire to touch Maddie. To be naked and in bed, with Maddie underneath her.

"I need you, Maddie," she said, her voice little more than a whisper. She reached out and tucked a lock of hair behind Maddie's ear as she spoke.

"Then what are you waiting for?" Maddie's voice was raspy, and her eyes fell to Savannah's lips for just a moment.

Savannah noticed the rapid rise and fall of Maddie's chest. She stood and held a hand out for Maddie. When they were facing each other, Savannah cupped Maddie's face in both hands, and ran a thumb across her bottom lip.

"There are so many things I want to do," she said with a slight grin. "But let's start with this."

The kiss was tentative at first, especially on Maddie's end, but Savannah used her tongue to urge her to let her in. As their tongues slid together, Savannah moved her hands slowly down Maddie's arms and then to her hips. She tugged at the tank top Maddie had tucked into her shorts, and when Maddie didn't object, she broke the kiss long enough to lift it over her head.

"My God, you're so beautiful," Savannah said, cupping the breasts she'd revealed. She met Maddie's eyes briefly before bending to take a nipple between her lips.

"Fuck," Maddie hissed as she held Savannah's head to her breast. "God, yes, just like that."

Savannah put one arm around her waist and pulled her even closer as she continued to suck on the nipple. Her other hand moved all over Maddie's bare torso as she marveled at how soft she was. After a few moments of this, Maddie gently pushed her away and reached for Savannah's shirt.

When they came together again, they both let out a groan at the first touch of skin on skin. Savannah's hands cupped her ass and lifted her, causing Maddie to wrap her legs around her waist as her arms went around Savannah's neck. It was difficult to concentrate with her breasts now at eye level, but Savannah managed long enough to ask one question.

"Should I wander around the house like this, or do you want to tell me where your bedroom is?"

Maddie directed her to the master suite but Savannah didn't release her until she'd gotten her on the bed. Savannah stretched out on top of her, and Maddie's legs went around her waist again.

"I really want to feel all of you," Savannah said into her ear. "Take your pants off."

They both made quick work of shedding their remaining clothes and then fell back together, as though there were magnets pulling them to one another. Maddie spread her legs to allow Savannah to settle in.

"You have no idea how long I've been wanting this," Maddie said, her hands moving up and down Savannah's sides and back. She finally settled them on her ass and pulled her hips closer as she thrust upward. "I really need you to fuck me, Savannah."

She didn't need to be told twice. Savannah lifted her hips just enough to slide her hand between their bodies, and as her fingers moved through the wet warmth she found waiting for her, she was alarmed to realize she was close to coming just from feeling Maddie. She held still for a moment and willed her body away from the edge before sliding two fingers inside.

"Oh, yes," Maddie said, her words strangled. Her head turned to one side as they began moving together, and Savannah ran her tongue along the smooth neck she revealed. "Please, Savannah, don't stop. You're going to make me come."

"Not yet," Savannah said in her ear before placing a kiss there. "I need to taste you first."

Maddie groaned loudly as Savannah pulled away from her and moved down her body, but she was taking her time exploring every inch of her. Maddie was impatient, which was obvious by the way she put her hands on Savannah's shoulders and urged her to move down farther. Savannah smiled against her skin before settling where she knew Maddie needed her.

Maddie's body tensed when Savannah ran her tongue the length of her sex and finished with a flick of her clit with her tongue. Maddie groaned again, and Savannah closed her lips around her clit, gently sucking as she thrust her fingers in rhythm with Maddie's movements. She kept up the steady motion when she felt Maddie begin to tighten around her fingers. Maddie dug her nails into her shoulders, and Savannah sucked harder until Maddie arched off the bed and cried out.

"Holy shit," Maddie said between gasps. Savannah worked her way back up her body to stretch out next to her, pressed against her side. Maddie turned her head to look at her. "You're really fucking good at that. I don't think I've ever come so fast before."

Savannah smiled but wasn't quite sure how to respond. She ran her fingers slowly back and forth across Maddie's stomach and raised herself up on an elbow. She should be freaking out about now, but she was strangely content to just lie there looking at Maddie. She moved her hand up to cup her cheek and leaned in to kiss her.

Maddie deepened the kiss as she slowly pushed Savannah onto her back and pushed one thigh between her legs. Savannah moaned deep in her chest and reached down to press the thigh tighter against her center. Maddie pulled her mouth away when she felt the wetness against her leg. She stared into Savannah's eyes and pressed harder when Savannah began to slide against her.

"I want to taste you," she said as Savannah's eyes closed. Savannah like this, her lips slightly parted, and her breath coming in ragged gasps might just have become Maddie's favorite look. She was so sexy.

"No," Savannah said, shaking her head. "I need to come now. Just like this. Kiss me while I come."

Maddie obliged, and when their tongues met, Savannah's movements against her leg became more frantic. She cried out as she turned her head away and Maddie changed her mind. Savannah's face as she orgasmed was most definitely her favorite look. And there was no doubt she wanted to see it again. And again, and again.

Chapter Twenty-three

M addie opened her eyes to a scratching at the bedroom door. She started to get up, but the arm thrown across her middle tightened, and the warm body next to her pressed against her back. She smiled at the memory of the night before. She could happily lie here in Savannah's arms for the rest of her life.

Unfortunately, Duke wasn't having it. He began to add whining to the scratching, and when he let out a high-pitched bark, Maddie knew she had to get out of bed or risk having to clean up a mess when she finally did get up.

"Don't go," Savannah mumbled against her shoulder.

"Duke needs to go out." Maddie managed to slide out of her grasp and stood, looking around the room at the array of clothes strewn everywhere. She shook her head and smiled as she pulled on her shorts. She leaned down and placed a kiss on Savannah's forehead. "Don't go anywhere. I'll be right back."

Savannah nodded, but never opened her eyes. Maddie tried her best to be quiet as she let herself out of the room and closed the door again behind her. She was surprised it was almost nine in the morning. Of course they hadn't fallen asleep until almost four, so it wasn't really too much of a shock.

She let Duke out and went to start a pot of coffee while she waited for him to let her know he was ready to come back in. They should probably have something to eat, but Maddie didn't know what Savannah liked for breakfast. Just as she was going to go let Duke back in, Savannah shuffled out of the bedroom, her shirt on inside out and backward. Maddie put a hand over her mouth to keep from laughing.

"What?" Savannah asked, her eyes only half open, and her hair tousled from sleep.

"You aren't a morning person, are you?"

"What gave it away?"

"You look like you got dressed with your eyes closed." Maddie closed the sliding glass door again and Duke ran straight for Savannah.

"I probably did," Savannah said with an ear scratch for Duke. "I usually don't get up much before noon during the season. Well, unless we have a morning practice scheduled."

"You didn't have to get up yet."

"Are you kidding?" Savannah asked, seeming to be more awake now. She grinned at Maddie, and Maddie felt her stomach flutter. "I need nourishment. You gave me one hell of a workout last night."

"I seem to recall you were the one who wouldn't let me fall asleep." Maddie was relieved this didn't seem to be awkward. Part of her expected Savannah would wake up this morning and regret what they'd done. She turned her back to Savannah to pour them each a cup of coffee.

"Can you blame me?" Savannah slid her arms around her waist and kissed her neck. "You're beautiful. I can't seem to keep my hands off you."

"Trust me, I'm not complaining." Maddie chuckled as she shook her head. This felt too good, too fast. Or was it? They'd spent as much, if not more, time together than a couple who had really been dating for five months. She closed her eyes and set the coffee pot down when Savannah's mouth closed over her ear lobe and sucked gently. "Fuck."

"Again?" Savannah whispered after she let go of the ear lobe. She moaned when Maddie pushed her ass back against her, causing a surge of desire to run through Maddie.

"Yes, please." Maddie turned in her arms and pressed her lips against Savannah's. Her hands were in Savannah's hair as Savannah's hands moved to her ass and pulled her body flush with hers.

"Why did we wait so long to do this?"

"Not my fault," Maddie said with a smirk. "You had a thing about sleeping with a neighbor, remember?"

"No." Savannah shook her head. "When you touch me I have a hard time remembering anything other than my name."

"Good to know," Maddie grinned. "I'll just have to make sure I keep touching you."

"I think that's an excellent idea." Savannah took a step back and grabbed her hand before pulling her toward the bedroom. "And I really think you should start right now."

"Okay, wait, so you're telling me you weren't really dating her?" Dana asked when Maddie called her not long after Savannah left in the afternoon. "It was all a ruse?"

"Yes, it's exactly what I'm telling you."

"But you slept with her last night." Dana seemed to be having a hard time grasping what was going on.

"Yes." Maddie was smiling. She hadn't been able to stop smiling. Savannah hadn't wanted to go, but she had to get to the arena for pregame warm-ups. Maddie still had some time before she had to leave. They hadn't discussed what exactly last night meant for them, but she was hopeful it meant there would be more touching and kissing in their future.

"And why exactly were you guys lying about it all this time?"

Maddie sighed before explaining—again—the reasons behind the lie. As she spoke, her mind returned to the bedroom and all that went on in there over the past sixteen hours or so. She felt the heat in her cheeks at the memory of Savannah climaxing at her hand. And her tongue. Numerous times.

"So what started out as fake has turned real?"

"I don't know, Dana. We didn't discuss it," Maddie said with a sigh.

"Why on earth wouldn't you have talked about it?"

"We were a little busy with other things." Maddie waited for her words to sink in, and Dana let out a chuckle almost immediately.

"Is she as good in bed as I imagined she would be?"

"Does your husband know you imagine Savannah Wells in bed?"

"Not exactly what I meant, Mads." Dana laughed, and Maddie could almost see her sister's face turning red. "I just meant she always seems so confident and self-assured. I imagine those qualities would carry over into the bedroom."

"Let's just say she's even better than I imagined she would be." Savannah grabbed an envelope off the kitchen counter and began to fan herself with it. She wondered if this was what hot flashes were like. "Let's leave it at that. And since we did not discuss what this means for us, I'd appreciate it if you wouldn't tell anyone."

"Except Trent, because you know damn well I'm going to tell him. I tell him everything."

"Fine, but neither of you can breathe a word about it. To anyone. I need you to promise me."

"Yeah, yeah, I promise," Dana said. "And I'll make Trent promise under threat of bodily harm."

"From who?" Maddie snorted, knowing Trent would never believe either of them would physically hurt him.

"Savannah, of course," Dana answered in a tone that indicated it should have been obvious. "He's in awe of how physical she is during games. I think he's a little afraid of her."

"Good. A little fear never hurt anyone." She glanced at the clock on the stove. "Listen, I should probably get ready for the game."

"Trent will be there with Amy. Make sure you say hi to him," Dana said. "And make sure you reiterate the threat of bodily harm."

They said their good-byes and Maddie let Duke out into the backyard for a few minutes before heading into the bedroom. She stopped just inside the door and stared at the bed for a moment, almost able to picture Savannah there, smiling at her. She indulged herself and went to lie down, her head on the pillow Savannah had used the night before.

She closed her eyes and breathed in her scent, an enticing combination of coconut and lavender. Savannah's face popped into her mind, and she smiled, feeling the throbbing between her legs start up once again, as it had so many times over the last several hours.

"Jesus," she murmured, but didn't open her eyes. She should have been completely satisfied after the things Savannah had done to her, but just the mere thought of her made Maddie want her again. She sat up quickly and went to her dresser to get the clothes she would put on after her shower. She knew if she'd stayed on the bed much longer she would have fallen asleep and had erotic dreams about Savannah Wells.

CHAPTER TWENTY-FOUR

Savannah didn't have anyone to talk to. Normally, she would have talked to Kelly about what had happened last night, but that option was off the table since Kelly didn't know they'd never slept together before. She suspected, yes, but there was no way she could know for certain. The second option would have been either Lisa or Faith, but the same reasons applied to them.

Why hadn't she and Maddie talked about what it all meant for them? Maybe Maddie was perfectly satisfied with a one-night stand. Savannah would have been. Before, but not now. Maddie was in her head, and had somehow woven her way into Savannah's heart. She felt lighter than she had in years. Her world finally felt *right*. She didn't know how else to explain it.

"You'd better get your head in the game, Wells," Kelly said with a quick shoulder bump.

"The game hasn't started yet," Savannah said. They were in the middle of warm-ups and they were stretching along the boards.

"Yeah, but I can tell your head is somewhere else."

"It's right here." Savannah looked at her and shook her head. "When have you ever known me to not be ready for a game?"

"I'm just saying." Kelly shrugged. She grabbed her stick and looked down at her. "Is everything okay with Maddie?"

"Perfect." Savannah tried to hide the goofy grin she knew she had, but Kelly's smile told her she hadn't been successful.

"Yeah," Kelly said as she tapped her on the leg with her stick. "We'll revisit that later."

Savannah watched her skate away, then glanced around at the stands. Her gaze lingered on Maddie, who was behind their bench talking with Trent and Amy. She was so incredibly beautiful. Especially when she laughed, which she was now at something Trent said to her. She sighed and got to her feet before grabbing her stick and joining her teammates for their shoot-around. At the last second though, she decided to skate to the bench for a different stick. Yeah, for a stick. Not to talk to Maddie.

"Hi," Amy said with a grin. Savannah gave a nod in her direction but quickly changed her focus to Maddie.

"Are you free after the game?" she asked, feeling uncharacteristically nervous. "We need to talk."

"Sure," Maddie answered, looking nervous herself. Savannah nodded again.

"Good luck tonight," Trent said.

"Thanks," Savannah answered, and she wondered if he was talking about the game, or the talk she and Maddie were going to have. Before heading back to her team, she held a stick out for Amy. "I'll get the whole team to sign it if you want."

"Wow, thanks!" Amy's eyes lit up, and Savannah's heart swelled. It always did when she'd done something to make a kid happy.

She gave Maddie one last look and saw she was smiling at her. It certainly didn't hurt to know she'd made more than one person happy with the gesture.

❖

Savannah was out for a rare penalty kill situation in the second period. She wasn't known for her penalty killing skills, but their regular winger in those situations was the one in the box. And the second line winger was out with an injury, so here she was.

Jen Hilton won the face-off and the puck came to Savannah, who headed up the ice. She passed it ahead to Hilton, who was a couple of steps ahead of everyone else. Hilton sent it back to Savannah as they both crossed the blue line and Hilton headed for the net. Hilton was to the left of the goaltender and was anticipating a pass, but Savannah saw the defender was too close to her. Savannah shot the puck instead of passing, and it went just over the goaltender's shoulder and into the top of the net.

Savannah knew Hilton was pissed when she didn't even come over to acknowledge the goal. The other two Warriors on the ice celebrated with Savannah by hugging and high-fiving. Hilton chose to return to the bench without a word. Savannah was congratulated by everyone on the bench while Hilton sat alone, quietly sulking.

"You should have passed it to me," Hilton said when Savannah took a seat next to her. "That was how the play was designed, Wells. That goal was supposed to be mine."

"Their defender was breathing down your neck," Savannah said, not even bothering to take her eyes off center ice where they were preparing for the face-off. Soothing egos wasn't her job. "I saw an opening and I took the shot. All that matters is we scored."

"No, all that matters is you're a puck hog."

"Is there a problem, ladies?" Gail asked as she came and stood behind them. Savannah simply shook her head and said nothing, while Hilton turned to look up at Gail.

"She's selfish, and I don't want her on the ice with me," she said, shooting a glare at Savannah.

"Grow up, Hilton." Savannah chuckled and shook her head. "We're part of a team. Maybe you need to learn what that means."

"We scored, ladies," Gail said. "It shouldn't be a reason for discord."

"If it makes you happy, next time I'll pass it to you and watch as they crash into you while you're facing the opposite direction," Savannah said when Gail walked away from them. "Maybe you'll be happier spending a few days on the injured list."

"You would be, wouldn't you?" Hilton turned her head to look at her, and Savannah did the same.

"Believe it or not, no, I wouldn't be," Savannah said. In all honesty, she'd be happy if Hilton never suited up for the Warriors again. She was nothing but trouble with a capital T, but she didn't want it to happen via injury. "I don't want anyone to get hurt, especially on my own team."

Savannah stood and jumped over the boards for her next shift, happy to leave Hilton behind. Not only was she homophobic, but she was also a drama queen. How anyone could thrive so much on conflict was beyond Savannah's comprehension.

When the game was over, they'd won by two goals, and Hilton had been held off the score sheet for the third consecutive game. She slammed her stick against the boards as she was coming off the ice, breaking it into three pieces. Savannah followed her into the locker room and wasn't surprised when Gail summoned Hilton to her office immediately.

"What the hell's her problem?" Alex asked as they all started getting undressed. "She wasn't like this last year."

"I have no idea, but for someone like her—someone who lives to stir up trouble—the drama always surfaces at some point." Kelly removed her pads and shoved them in her equipment bag. "She can't survive without it."

"I've never met anyone her age who was so immature," Savannah said as she grabbed a towel and headed for the shower. When she was finished, she saw Hilton just coming out of Gail's office, and she looked even more pissed than she had before.

"You feel like going out tonight?" Kelly asked when they were both dressed and ready to leave.

"No, I have plans," Savannah replied without looking at her.

"Too bad. I finally convinced Alex to go."

"Yeah, my boyfriend probably won't be too happy about me going to a lesbian bar." Alex chuckled and hoisted her bag over her shoulder.

"As long as he treats you right, I'm sure he's got nothing to worry about," Kelly said with a wink in Savannah's direction. Savannah shook her head with a sly smile. She knew Kelly would do her damnedest to give him something to worry about. She never much cared if a woman was gay or straight. They were all just another conquest to her.

"Behave yourself," Savannah said quietly so Alex couldn't hear. "Just remember she isn't someone you never have to see again. Hurting her wouldn't be a wise thing to do."

"You wound me," Kelly said, a hand over her heart. "I'm not stupid, you know."

"I do know, but sometimes your libido overrules your brain," Savannah chuckled and picked up her own equipment bag. "Just be careful, okay?"

"I always am." Kelly grinned before turning and walking out of the locker room behind Alex.

"Yeah, right," Savannah muttered under her breath. She glanced over at Hilton, who was glaring at her again, and she shook her head. She was not going to engage her. She was looking forward to seeing Maddie, and nothing was going to get in the way of that.

CHAPTER TWENTY-FIVE

Savannah went into her house to wait for Maddie, who had to go home and let Duke out. She kept telling her she could bring him over, but she was worried how he'd be with Leo. Savannah knew the scrappy little feline could take care of himself, hell, he dealt with all kinds of dogs when she took him to the vet's office. He never let any of them get away with anything. Maddie still worried though, and Savannah thought it was sweet.

She'd left the front door unlocked for Maddie and was in the kitchen getting them each a glass of wine when Maddie walked in. She handed her a glass and they went to get comfortable on the couch. Savannah took a deep breath.

"So, what was going on between you and Hilton on the bench after the short-handed goal you scored?" Maddie tucked a strand of hair behind her ear and took a sip of her wine. Hilton was the last thing Savannah wanted to be thinking about right now.

"She wasn't at all pleased I scored the goal and not her."

"Wow," Maddie said as she put her glass on the coffee table. "I got a few pictures of the two of you on the bench. I knew something set her off, but never thought it would be because you scored."

"It doesn't take much to set her off,' Savannah said with a shake of her head. She met Maddie's eyes and smiled. "But you know what? I really don't want to talk about her."

"Then what would you like to talk about?"

"Us. And what happened last night."

"You regret it." It was a statement, not a question, and the obvious hurt in Maddie's eyes caused a pain in Savannah's chest. Savannah moved so she was sitting right next to Maddie and took her hand, raising it to her lips.

"I do not regret any of it," Savannah said, trying to assure her. She tucked one foot underneath her and held Maddie's hand in her lap. "The only thing I regret is taking so long to act on my attraction to you."

"Yeah?" Maddie sounded skeptical, but her expression was hopeful.

"Yeah." Savannah gave a nod and reached out to cup Maddie's cheek. "I think we need to talk about what it means for us moving forward."

"I know you don't do relationships, and I know it was probably just a one-time thing," Maddie said with a shrug. "I'm okay with it."

"Really?" Savannah didn't believe her, and she was surprised to feel the pain again at Maddie's words. "Is that all you want it to be?"

"No..." Maddie said, her voice trailing off as she met Savannah's eyes. "But I know the deal, okay? I just want you to know I'm okay if last night was all we have."

"Well, I'm not," Savannah said, surprising herself when the words spilled out. Not surprised she felt that way, because she'd thought about little else all day. She was shocked she'd actually said the words out loud. She laughed at the expectant look on Maddie's face. "Believe me, no one's more stunned about it than I am. You're right. A relationship was the last thing I wanted, with you or anyone else. But then I got to know you."

"Okay, wait." Maddie sat back, obviously needing a little space between them to process this conversation. "Are you saying you want a *real* relationship now? With me?"

"Yes," Savannah said, knowing in the moment she'd never wanted anything more. She forced out a breath and shook her head, not believing this was really happening. "These past few months, I've really enjoyed spending time with you. You somehow found your way around the walls I'd put up, and you've managed to insert yourself into my life rather seamlessly. At this point, I honestly can't imagine my life without you in it."

"Wow," Maddie said, looking dazed. She squeezed Savannah's hand, then entwined their fingers. "You're serious? This isn't just some elaborate joke you and Kelly are playing on me, right?"

"It's no joke." Savannah hoped she sounded as sincere as she felt. "If you're willing, I'd really like to see where this might go."

"Are you kidding?" Maddie asked. "Of course I'm willing. Ready and able, too."

"Good to know." Savannah chuckled before leaning close and kissing her on the cheek.

"Are you really sure about this?"

"I am."

Maddie smiled and moved so she was straddling Savannah, both her hands cupping her face. "You're amazing. And beautiful. And sexy." She pressed her lips to Savannah's and moaned when Savannah moved her hands slowly up her sides, under her shirt. She pulled back and rested her forehead against Savannah's. "Did I mention sexy?"

"You did," Savannah answered with a grin.

"So damn sexy."

"You want to take this into the bedroom?"

"God, yes," Maddie said. She got to her feet and took hold of Savannah's hand. She followed Savannah as her heart was thundering in her chest. Was this really happening? She'd hoped their fake relationship might eventually lead to a real one, but she never thought it would actually happen.

Maddie's mouth went dry as she watched Savannah remove her clothes and stretch out on the bed. Savannah smiled and patted the mattress next to her.

"Are you waiting for an invitation?" she asked.

Maddie couldn't speak, so she shook her head in response as she tore off her own clothes. She got in the bed beside her, and Savannah immediately ran her fingers slowly up her torso, stopping only when she reached Maddie's nipples. Maddie let out a ragged breath and closed her eyes, enjoying the sensations Savannah's touch was causing.

"Jesus, Savannah," she said, her hand going to the back of Savannah's head when she took a nipple into her mouth. "I can't believe how you make me feel."

"How do I make you feel?" Savannah looked up and met her eyes briefly before returning her attention to the erect nipple.

"Special, sexy, alive. More than anything, you make me feel alive, Savannah," she said, her eyes closing again when Savannah moved lower and settled between her thighs. Maddie arched into her when she felt her warm tongue on her clit. "Yes. Right there, baby."

Savannah moaned against her and sucked lightly on Maddie's clit, causing her to buck involuntarily. Maddie spread her legs as far apart as she could and held Savannah's head in place. Her other hand gripped the sheet at her side and she did her best to make this last. She wanted to live in this feeling of anticipation for the rest of her life.

"Open your eyes," Savannah said, pulling her mouth away. Maddie whimpered at the loss of contact, but she did as she was told and looked into Savannah's eyes just as Savannah entered her. Her breath was labored, and her eyes slid closed again, but Savannah stopped her movements. "Maddie, look at me. I want to see you when you come."

Maddie tried her damnedest to keep her eyes open, but when she felt her inner walls tightening around Savannah's fingers, she lost the fight.

"Oh, my God, yes," she said, every muscle in her body beginning to spasm. "I'm coming, baby. You feel so fucking good, Savannah."

Her back arched off the bed and she cried out in a sound she'd never made before. It was primal, and she knew it was because she'd never been fucked like this before. Savannah was different from any woman she'd ever been with. Savannah cared about her, and it showed in the way she touched her.

When her body finally relaxed, she turned her head to the side and tried to even out her breathing. It wasn't working. Even though she felt like little more than a puddle, her heart was racing and she felt as though she were almost panting.

"Are you okay?" Savannah asked as she crawled up to lie next to her, her strong arms holding her close.

"I am most definitely better than okay," she said with a smile. She turned onto her side so her ass was pushed back against Savannah's front. She grabbed the arm around her and held it tight against her chest. "I think I need a minute or two to recover."

"Take your time," Savannah said into her ear. "I'm not going anywhere."

Maddie let out a sigh of utter contentment. Maybe what they were doing wouldn't last forever, but then again, maybe it would. All Maddie knew for certain was in this moment, with Savannah's arms holding her tightly, she was happier than she'd ever been in her life.

Chapter Twenty-six

They'd decided together to not tell Lisa and Faith the truth about their relationship, at least not until after Christmas. Dana was the only one who knew the truth, and if Savannah was being honest with herself, continuing to lie to Kelly and her moms was beginning to weigh on her. Savannah just wasn't sure she was quite ready to share so much yet. She was enjoying the time she was spending with Maddie, and every day she was falling more in love.

It was still scary as hell, but there was also a kind of peace she found in being with Maddie. They usually spent the night together, and on the occasional nights Savannah had to go out of town for a game, they still spoke on the phone. Now, about ten days out from Christmas, the Warriors were leaving on a three-day road trip, and Savannah wasn't looking forward to being away from Maddie for so long.

"We should tell them," Maddie said as Savannah parked the car. They were at Lisa and Faith's for Saturday brunch before Savannah had to catch the team bus later in the afternoon.

"You can't be serious," Savannah said. "You really want to tell them when I'm going to be leaving for a week? You know they won't let you hear the end of it, right?"

"You don't think I can handle myself?" Maddie's tone let Savannah know she was teasing.

"I know you're more than capable of handling yourself." Savannah chuckled as she released her seatbelt. "But I also know how relentless they can be."

"I'll be fine. If we tell them now, then by Christmas they'll be over it, right?" Maddie placed a hand on Savannah's thigh and squeezed gently. "No matter how we got to this point, we're together, so they should be happy."

Savannah had to agree. Maddie was making good sense. She finally shrugged because she couldn't think of any reason to not agree with her.

"Fine. We can tell them."

❖

"I can't believe you lied to us," Lisa said before they'd even sat down to eat. She was banging pots and pans around, which told Savannah she was really mad. She knew it was going to be this way. Savannah glanced at Faith for help, but Faith just shook her head and looked away without a word.

"Lisa, come on," Savannah said, trying hard not to get angry herself. Maddie squeezed her hand. "I asked you so many times to stop setting me up, and you never listened. Hell, you even talked Maddie into asking me out."

"Wait," Faith said, waving a hand in the air. She looked at Lisa. "You did what?"

"I did." Lisa turned to face the three of them as they stood there watching her. "I just want her to be happy, so if that makes me a horrible person, so be it."

"Honey," Faith said as she walked over to her and put her arms around Lisa. "You're not a horrible person. Nobody's saying that."

"Then why did she feel the need to lie to us?"

"Lisa," Savannah said, but Maddie cut in.

"It was my idea," she said, and Savannah looked at her like she was crazy. "It's true. I suggested it when you insisted I ask her out. I knew she hated being set up on blind dates, and I offered her a way to get it to stop. So if you're going to be mad at someone, it should be me. Not Savannah."

Savannah couldn't wait to get this entire ordeal behind them. She looked at the time, thankful the Warriors were leaving for their road trip soon. It couldn't come quick enough as far as she was concerned.

"There's no reason for anyone to be mad at anybody," Faith said. "No matter how it started, they're really dating now, so what does it really matter?"

"It doesn't," Lisa admitted. "But she's never lied to us before."

Savannah bit her tongue because she'd lied to them plenty when she and Noah had been teenagers. She sure as hell wasn't about to admit to it now though.

"Fine," Lisa said after a few moments of silence. She pulled herself away from Faith and went to hug Maddie. "I'm just so happy the two of you are together."

Maddie smiled at Savannah over Lisa's head, and Savannah let out a sigh as the tension finally left her body. She'd been dreading this conversation, but apparently it was all going to be okay. It seemed too easy.

"How long are we going to have Leo this time?" Faith asked as they were finishing their meal. They always took him when she went on the road with the team, and she'd brought him along with them this morning.

"I'll be back Friday," Savannah said. They were playing three games in the next six days. Most of the time when they played on the road it was only one overnight trip. This time they were going all the way to Chicago with a game in Columbus, Ohio, on the way there and one in Charleston, West Virginia, on the way back. She wasn't really looking forward to so many days on a bus, but such was the life of a semipro hockey player.

"Almost a whole week?" Faith asked.

"You want me to find someone else to watch him?"

"I can do it," Maddie suggested.

"No, Faith is just trying to be funny," Lisa said. "We love having him here."

"We should probably get going," Savannah said as she got to her feet. "I have a bus I need to catch."

They walked to the door and Lisa stopped her with a big hug before she could walk out. "I really am happy for you," she said with a kiss on Savannah's cheek. "I think she'll be good for you."

"Me too," Savannah said before kissing Lisa on the cheek as well. Faith gave her a clap on the shoulder with a wink and a nod, which was pretty much all the affection Faith ever showed. Savannah smiled at her when Lisa hugged Maddie again. "Okay, break it up. Gail will have my hide if I miss the bus."

They finally made it out of the house and were on the way to the arena with no time to spare. Savannah sent Gail a quick text to let her know she was on her way.

"We'll make it on time," Maddie assured her as she passed a couple of cars in front of them.

"Thanks for giving me a ride."

"You're welcome." Maddie smiled and put a hand on her thigh. "I'll pick you up when you get back too."

"You don't have to," Savannah said. "I can get a ride from Kelly."

"Seriously?" Maddie glanced at her. "I don't want to wait to see you until you make it to the house. I hate to think you're going to be gone so long as it is. I wish you were staying here."

Savannah stiffened in her seat and hoped Maddie didn't notice it. Was it happening already? Was Maddie seriously making demands on her time like Shauna had back in college? She couldn't deal with this right now. Not with the importance these next few games held as far as the standings went.

"What's the matter?" Maddie asked after a few minutes.

"Nothing," Savannah said with a shake of her head. She kept her eyes on the scenery outside the passenger window and silently willed Maddie to let it drop.

"Don't do that," Maddie said, sounding irritated. Savannah finally looked at her and saw the hurt in her eyes.

"Do what?"

"Shut me out. Something's obviously bothering you, and for some reason you think you can't tell me what it is."

"It's nothing," Savannah said, hoping she sounded more convincing than she felt. She forced a smile and placed her hand over Maddie's. "I'm just stressing over this road trip. The games are really important, you know?"

"Mm-hmm." Maddie nodded, but Savannah could tell she wasn't completely satisfied with her answer. She pulled into the arena parking lot and stopped right behind the bus. "Will you call me when you get to Columbus?"

"Yeah, sure," Savannah said. "I will."

"I'm going to miss you."

Savannah felt the smile she was still holding begin to fade, but she nodded and leaned over to give Maddie a quick kiss good-bye. She reached for the handle but stopped when Maddie gripped her arm.

"Are you sure there's nothing wrong?"

"I'm sure. I'll call you tonight, and I'll see you on Friday." The forced smile was still on her face, and Maddie must have believed it was real because she let her go.

"See you Friday," Maddie said as Savannah got out of the car.

She grabbed her bags out of the trunk of the car and waved at Maddie as she walked toward the bus. She tossed the bags into the storage area under the seats and let out a breath. She watched Maddie drive away before she boarded the bus and found a seat next to Kelly toward the back.

"About time you got here," Kelly said with a shoulder bump. "I thought Gail was going to leave without you."

Savannah didn't say anything in reply, but was completely lost in her own head. She'd thought she'd spent enough time with Maddie to discern she was nothing like Shauna, but she wasn't so sure now.

"Hey, Van," Kelly said quietly, leaning closer to her. "What's wrong?"

"Nothing," she replied with a quick shake of her head.

"Bullshit." Kelly stared at her a moment. "I know you, Van, and I sure as hell know when something's up with you. Spill."

"Can we talk later?" Savannah asked her, really not wanting to get into it now. They roomed together on the road, and she'd much prefer talking about this in private. Kelly was the only one who knew why things had gone to shit with Shauna, and she'd like to keep it that way.

"Yeah," Kelly said with a nod. "But I won't let you get out of it, so don't even think about it, all right?"

Savannah knew Kelly well enough to know the truth of her statement. Once she had something in her head, she was like a dog with a bone. She wouldn't let it go until she got the whole story.

CHAPTER TWENTY-SEVEN

S o, you were right," Savannah said as they were stretched out on separate beds in their hotel room after dinner. She'd called Maddie before they went downstairs to eat and was relieved she'd only gotten her voice mail. She left a quick message and then turned her phone off. Getting Kelly's take on the situation seemed more important at the moment than speaking with Maddie.

"Of course I was," Kelly said with a chuckle. "But to what are you referring?"

"When you said you didn't believe Maddie and I had ever slept together."

"I knew it." Kelly sat up and put her feet on the floor facing Savannah's bed. "But you did that night, didn't you? I could tell there was something different about you the next day. Wait, so this means you weren't really dating her, right? You lied to me?"

"We lied to everyone." Savannah turned her head to look at her. "It was to get Lisa to back off on the matchmaking. I wanted to tell you the truth, but I knew if I did, you'd never be able to keep it from her."

"Yeah, you're probably right. The woman scares the hell out of me." They both laughed and Kelly stretched out on her side, facing Savannah. "For some reason I never could lie to her."

"So you understand why I kept it from you."

"Absolutely. I would have done the same thing if I were you." Kelly watched her for a moment, and seemed to be figuring out what might be bothering her. "So you slept with her. What's the problem? Was she horrible in bed?"

"You're a dog, you know that?" Savannah laughed in spite of herself. Kelly always managed to make her laugh, no matter how bad things got in her life. She wasn't sure she'd have gotten through the whole Shauna ordeal if it hadn't been for Kelly there by her side the entire time, doing anything she could to make her laugh. "It's probably why you've never been in a relationship that's lasted more than a few hours."

"I beg to differ, my BFF," Kelly said with a grin. "It's because I don't want anything that's going to last until after the sun comes up."

"I don't believe you," Savannah said. "Even for all my bluff and blunder, I've always hoped there might be someone out there for me. Everybody wants something that will last."

"I'm not saying someday I won't find a good woman and settle down, but right here, and right now? I'm having way too much fun to even consider it."

"What if you've already met said *good woman,* but you don't realize it because you won't even consider it?"

"An interesting theory to ponder, I'll admit, but it hasn't escaped me that you haven't yet told me why you were so bummed when you got on the bus this afternoon."

Savannah stared at the ceiling for a few silent moments, trying to decide how to approach the matter. She decided the best way was to not even mention Shauna, but to see if Kelly jumped to the same conclusion she had.

"Maddie told me she wished I wasn't going on the road for the next week." Savannah waited, but Kelly didn't make a sound. She turned her head and saw Kelly watching her. "She didn't want me to go."

"Did she actually say she didn't want you to go? I mean, did she really say those words?"

"Well, no, but she did say she wished I wasn't going, and she hated I was going to be gone so long."

"Okay, so you guys weren't really dating, but then you slept together what…three weeks ago?" Kelly watched her as she waited for an answer and Savannah nodded, wondering where this was going. "I'm assuming it wasn't just the one time."

"No. We've been together pretty much all the time since then."

"I don't think it's a big deal, Van," Kelly said, sitting up again. "I mean, it's all brand-spanking new for the two of you. You know, the phase where you want to touch each other all the time. Where you can't stand to be apart for more than a few minutes. I think it's natural for her to feel that way. Don't start comparing her to Shauna already, okay? All you're going to accomplish is sabotaging what you might have before it even starts."

"Since you have no firsthand experience, how is it you can be so sure?"

"Just because I've never felt it, doesn't mean I don't know it exists," Kelly said, sounding defensive. "I do read, you know."

"Jesus, I know," Savannah laughed out loud. "My BFF, who is relationship-phobic, is a hopeless romantic addicted to lesbian love stories. It's really pretty hilarious if you think about it."

"Yeah, yeah, I'm laughing so hard I'm about to pee my pants," Kelly deadpanned accentuated with a dramatic eye roll, causing Savannah to laugh even harder. "Look, all I'm saying is you should give her the benefit of the doubt. Anyone who's been around you guys can see how much you both care about each other. It's sickening, really."

"Okay, fine," Savannah said, feeling surprisingly better about the entire situation than she had earlier. Thanks to Kelly, of course. "I'll give her the benefit of the doubt. But right now, I'm going to sleep."

"The hell you are," Kelly got to her feet and tried to force Savannah off her bed. "We're going out tonight. There's some unsuspecting woman out there who doesn't even know yet she's just waiting to meet me."

"I'm not going anywhere tonight, Kelly." Savannah turned away from her and curled into the fetal position. "We have an early morning skate tomorrow. Gail will hand us our asses if we show up hung over."

"You're no fun since you found a girlfriend." Kelly sounded as if she were pouting, but Savannah could hear the smile in her voice. "I'll stay in tonight, but tomorrow after the game, you're going out with me, understand? And I don't want to hear about how we have to be on the bus early in the morning, because we'll be on the damn bus all freaking day. We can sleep it off on the way to Chicago."

Savannah agreed, but she didn't really feel like going out. She just wanted Kelly to stop talking so she could go to sleep. There wasn't a whole lot of sleeping going on when she and Maddie slept together. The thought brought a smile to her face, and she drifted off before she even had a chance to change out of her clothes.

❖

"What the hell are you talking about, Dana?" Maddie asked, holding the phone tightly to her ear. This could not be happening. She'd missed Savannah's call while she'd been waiting for her sister to finish beating around the bush and to just tell her why she was calling.

"I'm sorry, Mads, I tried to tell her she wouldn't be welcome here, but you know how Mary is. How the hell did you put up with her for so long? I hope to God the sex was good."

"Jesus, Dana, I am not talking about this with you."

"Since when?" Dana laughed, which only caused Maddie to get even angrier. "You used to tell me everything."

"Mary," she said through clenched teeth. She was liking her decision to get a new phone and number even more now. "I'm not talking about my sex life with her because she doesn't matter to me anymore. At all."

"Okay, just calm down," Dana said, knowing as she always seemed to when Maddie was pissed off about something. "Listen, I didn't tell her where you live or anything, so there's no way she'll be able to find you."

"When is she coming?"

"Tuesday."

"You do realize she knows where you live, right?"

"Yeah, but Trent won't put up with any of her shit, you know that. He won't hesitate to call the cops if she shows up and refuses to go away."

"I'd like to see that." Maddie smiled at the thought. Mary would freak out if he called the cops to remove her from the property, but she knew Dana was telling the truth. Trent despised drama almost as much as Maddie did.

"Then come stay here with us for a few days. I'm sure Amy will be happy to hide you in her room and you can watch it all through the window."

"Don't tempt me. What the hell is she coming here for?"

"She wouldn't tell me. All she said was she needed to talk to you. To try and set things right between the two of you."

Maddie barked out a laugh and let her head fall back against the couch. Did Mary honestly think there was any way in the world to set things right? She'd be lucky if Maddie didn't strangle her on the spot. She'd told her when she left for Kingsville she never wanted to see her again, and Mary had assured her it wouldn't be a problem. So what could have happened to change all of that?

She couldn't possibly want to get back together, could she? No, there was no way. If it hadn't been bad enough for Maddie to have walked in on them in her own bed, Mary told her she'd never loved her. Those words had hurt far more than she ever let on to anyone, especially Mary. She would never have given her the satisfaction of knowing how much pain she'd caused.

"Mads, you still there?" Dana asked, sounding concerned.

"I'm here. I have to go. I'll call you tomorrow."

She disconnected the call and tossed her phone onto the couch next to her. She looked down at Duke, who was lying with his head on her lap. She stroked his side gently as he snored, and she couldn't help but smile. Yes, Mary had been the one who wanted him, but from the moment they'd brought him home, there was never any doubt he belonged to Maddie. Or rather, she belonged to him.

She couldn't go anywhere without him following on her heels, and if she sat down, he was right there on her lap. Until he got too big to fit comfortably on her lap, then he started lying next to her with his head on her lap, or on the floor with his chin resting on her feet. It had pissed Mary off so much.

Shit, what if she was coming to try to get him back? She'd be in for one hell of a fight if that was her plan. There was no way Maddie would allow her to take him. It would break Duke's heart as well as her own.

She looked at her phone and reached for it, remembering the missed call. She listened to the message Savannah left, but it didn't cheer her up. They hadn't left on good terms for some reason, and Maddie didn't want to let too much time pass before they could figure out what went wrong.

She sighed and closed her eyes when she was sent directly to voice mail. She hesitated for a moment, not sure she wanted to leave a message, but realized it would be rude. She hated when someone called and didn't leave a message.

"Hey, Savannah, it's me, Maddie." She rolled her eyes, knowing Savannah's phone would tell her who it was. Not to mention she hoped by now Savannah would recognize her voice. "I'm sorry I missed your call, but I was on the phone with Dana. Can you please call me when you get this? I really think we need to talk. I'm not comfortable with how we left things earlier. Anyway, I miss you, and I'll see you Friday. Bye."

She tossed the phone on the coffee table this time, startling Duke. She'd wanted to end the call with *I love you,* but neither of them had uttered those words yet. She was apprehensive to say it first, even though there was no doubt she was feeling it. She rubbed behind Duke's ears as he went back to sleep and she tried not to cry out in frustration. Just that morning, her life had seemed pretty perfect. Now it felt suspiciously as though everything was falling apart.

CHAPTER TWENTY-EIGHT

Savannah took a deep breath and readied herself for the face-off to begin overtime against the Columbus Wildcats. It had been a hard fought game, and regulation time ended in a 3-3 tie. She'd missed a few minutes late in the second period because she'd been in the locker room going through the concussion protocol. She'd taken a high-stick just after her helmet had popped off during a scrum in front of the net. The only solace she had was the puck went in off her stick to tie the game.

There hadn't been a penalty called even though everyone on the ice saw the woman from the Wildcats raise her stick fast and hard as she was looking right at Savannah. Well, not *everyone* it seemed. Otherwise the woman would have gotten a five-minute major and probably a game misconduct. Instead, she was now facing off against Savannah in overtime.

"Switch sides with me, Van," Kelly said as she skated over to her. She was looking at the woman as she spoke. "I'll take care of her."

"You need someone else to fight your battles, Wells?" The woman—Moore, according the name on her jersey—was someone they hadn't faced before. She laughed and shook her head.

"No, I don't," Savannah replied as she gave a pointed look to Kelly. "Get back to your own wing, Rawlins." Kelly stared at her for a few seconds, until the linesman blew the whistle to indicate he was ready to drop the puck. Savannah readied herself as Kelly went back to her position.

"Sorry I broke your pretty face," Moore said as she crossed her stick with Savannah's. Savannah didn't need to look at her to know she was smiling and didn't mean what she said. "Maybe next time you shouldn't camp out in front of the net."

Savannah said nothing while she moved the blade of her stick in front of Moore's. She wasn't going to give her the satisfaction of engaging with her. Moore moved her stick again at the same time she bumped Savannah with her hip. The linesman blew the whistle and moved toward them as Savannah took a couple of strides away from center ice. If Moore thought she was going to get under her skin, to get her to take off her helmet to fight, she had another think coming.

Moore followed her closely and shoved her from behind and Savannah stumbled, but stayed on her feet. She finally turned to look at Moore, and saw she'd dropped her gloves and took off her helmet. She was in a fighting stance and Savannah laughed at her as she held her arms out to the side to say *you want me, come and get me*. Moore took a swing but Savannah refused to duck, and her bare fist made contact with her helmet. Moore dropped to the ice holding her hand against her chest.

"You stupid bitch," Moore said as Kelly came and stood facing Savannah, moving her back toward the bench.

"Are you all right?" Kelly asked. She looked back over her shoulder as the Wildcats' trainer came out to escort Moore back to the locker room.

"I'm fine," Savannah said, pulling away from her.

"Oh, hell no," Savannah heard Gail say from the bench behind her. She looked up at the scoreboard and saw they'd both been given two minute minor penalties.

Kelly tried to stop her, but Savannah broke away again and skated fast across the ice to confront the referee. She stopped right next to him and took her helmet off.

"What the hell?" she asked, pointing to her cheek, which hadn't actually been broken. Just a cut that had required stitching and she was sure there was a nice bruise by now as well. "You missed the call on the high-stick, which was blatantly obvious, and now you're giving me a penalty? For what? She took a swing at me, and I just stood there. I did nothing."

"You taunted her, and you had plenty of time to get out of the way of her swing," the ref said without looking at her. He calmly skated toward the bench to explain what was happening as a courtesy to the two coaches. Savannah tried to follow him, but one of the linesmen got in her way and turned her back toward the penalty box.

"This is bullshit!" Savannah yelled as the linesman shoved her into the box. As the referee skated to his position, she slammed her stick against the plexiglass, causing the stick to break. She sat down as the ref made the motion for a ten-minute misconduct. She was livid when both linesmen came to escort her back to the bench where she'd return to the locker room. She was done for the night. She couldn't even remember what expletives she'd spewed at the officials. It took two players to get her off the bench and down the walkway toward the locker room.

She threw her equipment into her bag as she got undressed and grabbed a towel for her shower. She heard the crowd erupt, indicating the Warriors had lost the game. She showered quickly and was sitting in front of her locker fully dressed as the rest of the team was heading for the showers.

"Savannah, can I have a word?" Gail asked from behind her. She was expecting this, so she stood and followed Gail to the office, closing the door behind them.

"It was a shitty call," Savannah said as she took a seat.

"It was for unsportsmanlike conduct, and I have to agree with the call," Gail said, shaking her head. She held a hand up when Savannah was about to argue. "Let me finish. I agree they blew the call earlier when you took a stick to the face. You have a really nice bruise there, by the way. But it was over and done with. You *did* taunt her. If you hadn't done what you did, maybe she wouldn't have thrown the punch."

"That's bullshit, and you know it. She was itching for a fight."

"Maybe, maybe not." Gail shrugged. "Either way, you should have just skated back to the bench and completely ignored her."

"She shoved me from behind, Gail," Savannah said in an attempt to justify her actions. She was trying hard to ignore the ache high up on her cheekbone, just below her right eye. "Yes, you're probably right, but look at what she did to me, for fuck's sake. I had to get twelve stitches to close this. Then she just kept pushing me, and I did ignore her until she shoved me. I'm only human, Gail. Tell me you wouldn't have reacted to it."

"I can't tell you that." Gail sighed and ran a hand through her hair. She shook her head and looked Savannah in the eye. "You're coming with us to Chicago, but you're sitting out the game."

"Why?"

"Looking at your face right now, you probably shouldn't have come back in this one, but I listened to you when you said you were ready to go."

"I was ready." Savannah stood and walked to the door. With her hand on the knob, she glanced back at Gail. "I'm fine to play."

"I'll think about it," Gail said after a few seconds, but Savannah knew once she'd made up her mind, Gail rarely changed it.

Savannah went right to Kelly and placed a hand on her shoulder as Kelly was tying her shoes.

"I'm not going out drinking tonight."

"Yeah, I figured." Kelly grinned at her. "Damn, that's a fancy shade of purple."

"Fuck off," Savannah said good-naturedly as she shoved her. "I'm just going back to the hotel and get some sleep. You can go out if you want. Don't worry about me."

❖

Savannah still hadn't spoken with Maddie since she'd left, and a part of her didn't even want to turn her phone on. She knew there'd be messages from her, and she didn't feel like dealing with any of it tonight. But she knew Lisa and Faith had listened to the game on the radio because they always did, and they would no doubt be worried about her. She had to turn her phone on so she could call them.

Just as she suspected, there were four voice mails, and more than a few texts, all from Maddie, and all imploring her to call. She decided she would, after calling her moms.

"Lisa's going crazy," Faith said when she answered her call. "It's a good thing you called."

"I figured." Savannah chuckled. "I'm fine. A cut and a bruise. No big deal."

"Yeah, I think she was more worried about the profanity laden tirade you went on after getting your misconduct penalty."

"Not my finest moment," Savannah admitted with a sigh.

"Are you going to get a suspension for it?"

"I wouldn't be surprised. These officials were assholes." Savannah closed her eyes and leaned her head back against the pillows she'd propped up on her bed. A suspension wasn't something she'd even considered, and even though she didn't remember the bulk of what she'd actually said in the heat of the moment, she supposed she did verbally abuse the officials, which was grounds for suspension. What a perfect end to an utterly horrible weekend it would be.

"What's going on with you and Maddie?" Faith asked, her voice not much more than a whisper, which Savannah assumed was so Lisa couldn't hear the question. "She called here earlier and wanted to know if we'd heard from you. I didn't tell Lisa she called."

"It's nothing," Savannah said, closing her eyes again. She was a horrible liar but thought maybe it would be easier over the phone, when she wouldn't have to look the other person in the eye as she lied. "I'm going to call her when I hang up with you."

"Well, I don't believe you, but as long as you work things out, I guess it doesn't really matter. You know you can talk to me about anything, right?"

Savannah nodded even though she knew Faith couldn't see her do so. She felt tears welling up, but she swallowed them down. Why hadn't she ever confided in Faith about what happened with Shauna? It was the one big regret she had in life.

"I do know, and I love you for it," she finally managed to say.

"All right. I'll tell Lisa you're fine, and we'll see you when you get back on Friday." Faith sighed. "I love you, Vanna."

"You're such a dork," Savannah said with a laugh. They hung up and Savannah stared at her phone, dreading the next call she had to make. She half expected Maddie to call before she had the chance. She took a deep breath and pushed the button to call her. She answered after only the second ring.

"Thank God, Savannah, where have you been?"

"I left a message last night, then I turned the phone off so I could get some sleep," Savannah said. "I completely forgot it was off until I got back to the hotel after the game tonight. I'm sorry."

"I'm just glad you're okay," Maddie said with a sigh of what Savannah assumed was relief. "Or are you? I listened on the radio tonight. What happened?"

"I took a stick to the face. It's just a cut and a bruise." Savannah sat up and put her feet on the floor. "It's one of the hazards of playing hockey."

"I thought they were supposed to blow the whistle if someone's helmet comes off."

"It happened pretty fast. There was a scramble in front of the net and somehow it came off, and the next thing I knew, I was on the ice and there was blood all over the place."

"But you're okay now?"

"I'm fine, Maddie," Savannah said, even though she was starting to get one hell of a headache. "I might not play the next game though, and there's a possibility of a suspension because I said some pretty nasty things to the officials. I might need you to pick me up before Friday if that happens."

"Just let me know, and I'll be there whenever you need me to be," Maddie said, but Savannah thought she sounded reluctant. She decided not to ask her about why.

"I need to go," Savannah said after a moment. "We have to be on the bus early in the morning, and I really need to get some sleep."

"Oh, okay." Maddie was disappointed, that much was obvious. "Are we okay?"

"Of course we are," Savannah said, remembering what Kelly had said the night before about being in the *can't keep your hands off each other* phase, and hoped they really were okay. "I'll call you if I'm coming home before Friday."

They ended the call with both of them saying they missed each other, which caused the worry to grow in the pit of Savannah's stomach again, but she did her best to ignore it. Kelly was probably right, and there was nothing to fret about. Everything she'd learned about Maddie in the past few months led her to believe she was nothing at all like Shauna, and she clung to the thought as she tried to fall asleep.

CHAPTER TWENTY-NINE

Maddie really had no choice but to believe Savannah when she'd said they were okay. She hadn't sounded upset about anything when they'd spoken the other night, but Maddie couldn't get rid of the sense something had gone wrong between them somewhere between leaving Faith and Lisa's and when she'd dropped her off at the bus Saturday afternoon. She tried to shake the feeling off, and tried to convince herself everything would be all right when Savannah got back.

But right now, she was dreading the fact Mary was going to turn up at Dana's house sometime today. Part of her wanted to just hide away at home and try to avoid her until she gave up and returned to Chicago, but the more mature part of her knew she should just find out what Mary wanted and get it over with.

Dana was going to call her when Mary showed up, so there was no point in sweating about it until she got the call. Hell, it was almost four o'clock now, so maybe she'd changed her mind about coming. She threw on a sweatshirt and took Duke out into the backyard to expend some of his energy by playing fetch with a tennis ball. By the time he brought it back for the third time, her phone began vibrating in her pocket. She tossed the ball one more time before swiping the screen to answer.

"Hi, Dana," she said. "I take it she's arrived?"

"She has," Dana replied with a sigh.

"Did she tell you what she wants?"

"She wants to talk to you. She's offered to buy us all pizza if you'll come over for dinner."

"Damn it, I have nothing to say to her, Dana." Duke dropped the ball at her feet and sat as he looked up at her, his tail wagging. She threw it again before turning and going back into the house. "Did you tell her that?"

"I did. She's being really nice, Mads, it's kind of creepy."

"Of course she's being nice. She wants something."

"What could it hurt to come over here for dinner? We'll all be here too, so it isn't like anything bad is going to happen."

"Fine. I'll be there at six." Savannah disconnected and resisted throwing her phone against the wall in the kitchen. She leaned forward with her elbows on the counter. She usually took Duke with her when she went to Dana's, but she wasn't going to do it tonight. Maddie wasn't completely sure Mary wasn't here to try to take Duke back, so she wasn't going to risk him being there and vulnerable.

She sighed and headed to her room to get dressed but stopped when she heard Duke whining at the back door. She let him in and sat on the couch with him for a few minutes, telling him how much she loved him, and how she was never going to let Mary take him away from her. He stared at her as she spoke, his head tilted to one side as if he actually understood what she was saying.

"You're such a good boy, Duke." She held his face in her hands and kissed him on the snout. She took a deep breath as she stood. Might as well get it over with.

"Hi, Trent," Maddie said when he opened the front door to let her in. She looked into the living room but didn't see anyone.

"She's in the kitchen with Dana," he said, obviously able to read her mind. "Where's Duke?"

"He never really liked Mary, so I left him at home."

"He has good taste."

"I should have taken the hint when he attached himself to me after she brought him home. Dogs are good judges of character."

She gave him her jacket to hang up, then followed him into the kitchen. When she saw Mary standing there talking to Dana, Maddie wanted to strangle her. How dare she show up here after what she'd done to her? She took a deep breath and then plastered on her best fake smile before going to hug her sister.

"Hi, Maddie," Mary said. When Maddie looked at her, she could tell Mary was going to try to hug her too, so she put a hand up and stepped back. "It's good to see you again."

"Wish I could say the same." Maddie folded her arms over her chest and leaned her hip against the counter. "What are you doing here, Mary?"

"I just wanted to see you."

"Why?" Maddie could feel herself starting to shake, but she thought she was doing a good job of hiding it. "I'm pretty sure we didn't end things amicably, and I seem to remember telling you I never wanted to see you again. And to ensure that, I moved here."

"Can we talk please?" Mary asked, strangely calm. Maddie was surprised because Mary was always quick to lose her temper. The woman standing before her was at odds with the woman she once knew. "In private?"

"Whatever you have to say you can say in front of Trent and Dana. It will save me the trouble of having to tell them everything later."

Mary shifted her weight from one foot to the other as she stared at her feet, refusing to meet anyone's gaze. Maddie almost felt sorry for her, but then she recalled Mary's infidelity and subsequent claim she'd never loved Maddie, coupled with the possessive way she treated her, and her anger was instantly back.

"Fine," Mary said with a sigh. She looked at Maddie with some of her old defiance. "I want you back, Maddie. My life is so empty without you. I came here to convince you to come home with me."

Maddie barked out a laugh. She couldn't help it. Did she really think there was a chance in hell Maddie would go back to her? She knew she was standing there with her eyes wide and her mouth hanging open, but there wasn't anything she could do about it. Maddie was that shocked by her statement.

"I think it's pretty safe to say it is not going to happen," Dana said, looking at Maddie as though she was worried about her. She squeezed Maddie's arm, and that seemed to bring her out of her stupor.

"Never," Maddie said, shaking her head. "Not in a million years, and not if you were the last woman left on earth."

"At least say you'll think about it," Mary said. Trent laughed this time, but he didn't say anything.

"I don't need to think about it," Maddie said, trying her best to keep her voice at an even keel. "You cheated on me. You. And, I might add, you made it pretty clear you were never in love with me. You wouldn't let me have friends of my own or even go anywhere without you, so why the hell would I even consider going back to you? Have you lost your mind in the months since it all happened? Or did your new girlfriend dump you because you cheated on her too? You've got a lot of nerve."

"Mom, Dad, I'm home!" Amy yelled as the front door slammed shut. She was just getting home from basketball practice. "The game's on at eight tonight because the Warriors are in Chicago. Oh, and Aunt Maddie's girlfriend did not get suspended."

Maddie cringed as she felt Mary's eyes boring into her. She'd never planned to tell Mary she was seeing anyone, mostly because it had nothing to do with her. Mary's face was turning red. At least the Mary she knew was finally making herself known, though she had absolutely no reason to be pissed. They were done.

"Girlfriend?" she asked, her voice tight. Trent left the room, no doubt to stop Amy from coming into the kitchen. "You have a girlfriend?"

"Yes, she does," Dana answered for her. "And they're very much in love, so I suggest you go back to Chicago and get on with your life."

"What's her name?" Mary asked, completely ignoring Dana.

"It's none of your fucking business, Mary." Maddie gritted her teeth.

"This isn't over," Mary said, stepping close to Maddie. "I'm here through the end of the week, so don't think I'm just going to go away. I'm taking Duke back with me. He was my dog before you stole him."

"He's not going anywhere with you. He doesn't even like you." Maddie followed her out of the kitchen toward the front door.

"We'll see how true that is when he sees me." Mary grabbed her coat from the closet and slammed the door before turning back to Maddie. "Obviously, it was a mistake coming here, but I thought you'd appreciate the grand gesture being the hopeless romantic you are."

"You don't know me at all." Maddie opened the front door for her to make her exit easier. "Leave me the hell alone."

Mary laughed as she walked out the door, but Maddie slammed it as soon as she crossed the threshold. She rested her forehead against the door, her eyes closed. She was so angry she wanted to punch something, but since Mary was the only thing she *really* wanted to punch, she took a deep breath and tried to calm her racing heart.

"You've never referred to Savannah as Aunt Maddie's girlfriend," she heard Trent saying to Amy, and Maddie felt a laugh bubbling up from her chest. "Why tonight, of all nights?"

"I saw her car in the driveway," Amy said, sounding panicked. "I only said it to tease her. I didn't know Mary was here."

"It's okay," Maddie said, finding the entire situation humorous for some reason. She supposed it was simply the relief washing through her that Mary was gone. She turned and walked to Amy, gathering her in her arms for a hug. "It isn't your fault, honey."

"I'm still sorry," Amy said, speaking into Maddie's shoulder.

"So, Savannah wasn't suspended?" Maddie asked as she pulled away from her and kissed her forehead. She wondered why Savannah hadn't called and told her about it, but she didn't dwell on it.

"Yeah, but that's all I heard." Amy put an arm around her waist as they followed Dana back to the kitchen. "I'm sure they'll talk about it on the radio tonight."

Maddie nodded. She couldn't wait for Friday when she could see Savannah again.

CHAPTER THIRTY

S avannah sat in the stands for their game in Chicago because Gail benched her as an example to the rest of the team. She didn't really mind though, because she was able to sit with Lana who was there on a night off from the orchestra she played in.

"So what happened in Columbus?" Lana asked when she sat down before the start of the game. She turned in her seat to look at her and smiled. "Nice colors, by the way. Does it hurt?"

"It looks a lot worse than it feels, to be honest." Savannah touched her cheekbone lightly and shook her head.

She explained everything that went down in the previous game, pausing a few times to watch the action on the ice before them. They were sitting right behind the team benches which gave Savannah great access to hear what was going on.

"Court said you were probably facing a suspension," Lana said when play stopped for an offside call. "Don't take this the wrong way, but why didn't you get one?"

"The head of officials was present for the game, and he saw everything, including the high-stick the on-ice officials missed," Savannah said, remembering back to earlier in the day when Gail told her about it. "Yes, I taunted her, and yes, I verbally abused the officials, but they understood my frustrations. Because I'd never been disciplined before, they gave me a warning this time. But the kicker is the referee has been suspended for three games."

"Wow." Lana nodded her head in approval. "Well, congratulations. Why are you sitting out tonight then? Is your injury worse than the team's letting on?"

"Nah," Savannah said, shaking her head. She watched as Hilton skated in on the goaltender and sent a wrist shot in that was easily turned away. *I would have scored on that play. Most of the team would have.* She wondered, not for the first time, what the brass saw in Hilton. She really wasn't that good of a player. Savannah turned her attention back to Lana. "I woke up with a pretty nasty headache yesterday morning, and even though they put me through the concussion protocol during the game, they looked me over again. No concussion, but they thought it would be best for me to sit out a game."

"It's good they're erring on the side of caution," Lana said.

"I suppose, but I'd really rather be out there," Savannah said, then she realized how it sounded. "No offense. Honestly, if I had to miss a game, this is where I'd want it to be. At least I have you to keep me company."

"None taken." Lana chuckled. They watched the game in silence for the rest of the period, which ended with the Wolves up by two. Lana turned her body slightly to face Savannah. "How are things with you and Maddie?"

Savannah hesitated before answering, and realized it was a mistake. The look of concern on Lana's face was obvious. She looked down at her hands and sighed.

"What's going on?" Lana asked, a hand on Savannah's knee. "You know you can talk to me, right? I promise I won't say anything to Maddie if you don't want me to."

"I'd appreciate it if you didn't," Savannah said, meeting her eyes. "It just goes back to an old hang-up I have about relationships. It's nothing serious."

"You'll forgive me if I'm skeptical, because your demeanor says it is a big deal."

Savannah wasn't sure why, but she told Lana everything. She was just so easy to talk to, and she now understood why Court had fallen so hard for this woman. She was happy for Court, and for Lana too, and she'd be lucky if she could someday find the same kind of love. She'd found herself believing it might be with Maddie, but she wasn't so sure now.

"I can see why your guard would be up," Lana said. "But with everything I know about Maddie, she isn't the type to look elsewhere. Her ex cheated on her, and she's told me it's the one thing she could never forgive. If Maddie's with someone, I don't see her cheating. I think it might just be she wasn't looking forward to being apart from you for a whole week because things are so new between the two of you."

"Kelly said basically the same thing."

"I think if you'll look deep inside yourself, you'll agree with both of us. Am I right?"

"Yes," Savannah said, somewhat reluctantly. It wasn't so much she didn't want to agree, it was simply because she wasn't sure she could trust her own instincts any more. She should have realized on her own it was due to the newness of their relationship, and not anything to be worried about, without having other people pointing it out. "See? I told you it was nothing serious."

"But it could be if you allowed it to keep eating away at your thoughts." Lana turned back toward the ice as the Wolves returned to their bench. Court waved at Lana and smiled, before sending a nod in Savannah's direction.

Savannah settled in and readied herself for the second period. She found herself looking forward to returning home on Friday and seeing Maddie. She smiled to herself just as Jen Hilton looked at her, a frown on her face. Savannah stuck her tongue out at her quickly before turning her head away and smiling again. It was childish, yes, but it gave her a certain amount of satisfaction.

The Warriors lost the game to the Wolves, and it was the first time in two seasons they'd dropped two games in a row. Gail wasn't happy, and she let the team know it. She called out Jen Hilton for her abysmal giveaways in their own zone which led directly to two of the Wolves' goals. As usual, Hilton was in a surly mood after being singled out, and no one wanted to be anywhere near her.

Savannah was back in the lineup for the game in Charleston two nights later, but she saw limited ice time because Gail didn't want her suffering any further injury with a big home stand coming up when they returned. Even with reduced playing time, Savannah managed to score two goals in the win.

They made good time on the ride back to Kingsville, which was good because a major snowstorm was forecast. They arrived almost an hour before they were scheduled to. Getting there early caused all kinds of problems for the people who had arranged to have someone pick them up. Not to mention the fact it was snowing like a bitch. There were at least two inches on the ground already.

"My truck's here," Kelly said, pointing toward the lot in back of the building. "I can give you a ride home if you want to save Maddie the trouble."

"Yeah, probably not a bad idea," Savannah said as they began walking. She pulled out her phone and found Maddie's number. It only rang once before she answered.

"Hey, you," Maddie said, and Savannah was surprised at the surge of excitement coursing through her body at the sound of her voice.

"Hey," Savannah said, lowering her voice and slowing down so she was a couple of steps behind Kelly. "Listen, we just got to the arena, and I'm going to catch a ride with Kelly. I should be home in about twenty minutes."

"Oh, okay." Maddie sounded a little disappointed. "I'm at Dana's right now."

"Don't rush home, all right? The roads don't look too good right now," Savannah said. She waited while Kelly opened the back of her SUV so they could throw their bags in. "When did this start?"

"Just a couple of hours ago. They say we might end up with a foot or more before it's over by tonight."

"As much as I want to see you, maybe you should stay at Dana's for the night," Savannah said, hoping Maddie would listen to her and not risk getting stuck somewhere. "I'll pick you up there tomorrow."

"Dana's been telling me the same thing so I guess I will, but I really want to see you."

"Me too." Savannah got in the passenger side and buckled herself in as she held the phone between her ear and her shoulder. "I've missed you more than you know, but one more night won't make too much difference, right?"

"I suppose you're right," Maddie said quietly, and Savannah imagined Dana and probably Amy were close by. "I can't wait to see you."

"Neither can I," Savannah said with a sigh. Since she'd decided to give Maddie the benefit of the doubt, she'd really been looking forward to seeing her again. They talked for a couple more minutes before they hung up. "She's at her sister's. I talked her into staying there for the night."

"I gathered as much from what I heard," Kelly said, leaning forward to try to see the road better. "I'm thinking I might just crash at your place if it's all right with you."

"Of course." Savannah tried to think of whether or not she had any food in the house, and came to the conclusion she did not. At least not enough for more than one person. "You think we could make a pit stop at the grocery store for supplies?"

"No problem."

They made it to the store without any major difficulties, but the parking lot was so empty, Savannah worried maybe they were closed. Kelly let her out at the front door so she could make sure they were open. When the automatic door opened, she waved at Kelly to indicate she should park the SUV.

She was at the butcher counter to get a couple of steaks when a woman walked up to her and smiled. Savannah smiled back, knowing she probably looked frightful with the huge bruise and stitches on her cheekbone.

"Hi, you're Savannah Wells, right?" the woman asked.

"I am," she replied as the butcher handed her the package he'd gotten ready for her. She turned and faced the woman then. "Do I know you?"

"No, but we have a mutual...friend." The woman smiled again and Savannah cocked her head to the side, waiting for her to elaborate. If this was one of Kelly's one-night stands, she was going to kill her BFF. "My name's Mary."

"Okay, I'm sorry, but that doesn't help."

"Don't tell me Madison never mentioned me," Mary said, and it all became clear. This was the ex. Savannah shook her head and started to walk away from her, but Mary put a hand on her forearm. "Don't go, please. I think we need to talk."

"I have nothing to say to you."

"Are you sure about that?" Mary raised an eyebrow as she asked the question.

Savannah decided she would listen to what Mary had to say but wouldn't put any credence in her words. She resisted the urge to look around for Kelly and kept her eyes squarely focused on Mary.

"See, the thing you have to understand about Maddie's and my relationship is we always have these falling outs," Mary said as she urged Savannah to move away from the butcher counter. "One of us always leaves, and the other always goes to find the one who left. It took me a few months to figure out she'd actually left Chicago this time, but I finally found her. She'll be going back with me, so I'm sure you'll understand when I ask you to stay away from her."

"Are you through?" Savannah asked after a moment.

"Yes, I think I've said everything I needed to say."

"Then I'd appreciate it if you'd please leave."

"Oh, there is one more thing," Mary said, her hands on her hips. "Maddie isn't the kind of woman you leave alone for an entire week while you're off playing a game. She gets to feeling neglected, and well, she might look for companionship elsewhere, if you know what I mean."

"Enough," Kelly said as she stepped up to stand next to Savannah.

Savannah's pulse was pounding in her head, making it difficult to hear what was being said, but it was obvious Kelly was giving Mary an earful. Savannah started to feel light-headed, and she turned to walk away from them to lean against the butcher counter for support. She knew she shouldn't believe a word Mary said, and she silently cursed Shauna for doing such a number on her. Or maybe it had been her own damn fault. She knew she needed to talk to Maddie, but right now, she just needed some time to think.

"Come on, Van, let's go," Kelly said, gripping her elbow and leading her away from Mary. "You know you can't believe a word she said, right?"

"Yeah, I know," Savannah said.

"I'm taking you home, but we have one more stop to make along the way," Kelly said. When Savannah looked at her questioningly, Kelly shook her head. "The beer store."

Chapter Thirty-one

S avannah opened her eyes but didn't move her head. She didn't think she could with the way it was pounding. Plus, there was a body pressed against her back, and an arm around her torso, holding her tight. Her heart began to race. She remembered Kelly bringing her home the night before, and they ate dinner, then started in on the twelve-pack of beer they'd bought. She was pretty sure they finished it off, and drank the few bottles she'd already had in the fridge when they ran out.

Fuck, she thought as she swallowed hard. Had she slept with Kelly? There was no doubt it was her pressed against her, but why? She closed her eyes and took a deep breath before looking down and seeing she still had all her clothes on. *Thank God.*

She groaned as she tried to extricate herself from Kelly's grasp, but Kelly tightened her hold on her and sighed. It soon became clear she was going to have to wake Kelly up if she really wanted to get out of the bed.

"Kel," she said, but it came out little more than a croak. She cleared her throat and tried again. "Kelly, come on, I have to pee."

"What?" Kelly said, then groaned herself as her own hangover must have made itself known. Savannah was happy she wasn't the only one. "Shit. What the hell happened?"

"I have no idea." Savannah slowly got to her feet and looked down at Kelly, who was also completely clothed, just minus the sweatshirt she'd been wearing. At least she'd had a tank top on underneath it. "I think it's safe to say we both got shit-faced last night. I need water."

"And aspirin," Kelly said, sounding weak. "Lots and lots of aspirin."

Savannah finished in the bathroom and made her way to the kitchen to make some coffee. She heard Kelly rummaging around in her bedroom and then the shower coming on. She was sitting on the couch with her coffee when Kelly finally emerged from the bedroom.

"You're my hero," Kelly said, pouring herself a cup of her own and finding the aspirin Savannah had set next to the coffee maker.

"Why were you in my bed with me?" Savannah asked when Kelly joined her on the couch.

"You asked me to stay," she said, her head resting on the back of the couch and her eyes closed. She chuckled. "I don't remember much of last night, but I do remember that. You didn't want to be alone. You know you're the only woman I've ever woken up with in the morning?"

"We didn't…you know?" Savannah knew Kelly would understand what she asking.

"No, we didn't," Kelly said, chuckling. "Even drunk we both know we're just friends, and not friends with benefits."

Savannah's phone was sitting on the coffee table and it began vibrating, skittering a few inches away. She reached for it but saw Maddie's name on the display and quickly pulled her hand back. Her encounter with Mary the previous day came rushing back to her.

"Fuck, I can't talk to her," she said, glancing at Kelly.

"You're supposed to pick her up today." Kelly got up and walked to the front window, pulling the curtain back so she could see outside. "I don't think you'll be doing that without a four-wheel drive though. I could go get her if you want. I could tell her you aren't feeling well because of your cheek."

Savannah thought about it for a moment, then decided it might not be a bad idea. Kelly was brash sometimes, but she could be discreet when she needed to be. She doubted Kelly would let on about what had happened in the grocery store, and that would be for the best as far as Savannah was concerned. She needed time to process things. She knew she shouldn't take Mary's word for anything, but her old insecurities were playing a huge part in her current way of thinking.

"I'd really appreciate that," she said when Kelly came and sat down again. "You won't tell her about Mary, right?"

"Hell no, it's between you and her. I can buy you some time though, so maybe she won't try to see you until tomorrow."

"I'm so happy you're my best friend," Savannah said with a grin. Her stomach growled, and she realized her headache had subsided enough to consider getting some food into her belly. Nothing too fancy though. "Want some toast?"

"That's all you have to offer your best friend?"

"I think it's all I can handle at the moment. If you want anything else, you'll have to make it yourself."

❖

Maddie was surprised when she looked out the window and saw Kelly pulling into the driveway of her sister's house. She saw there was no one in the passenger seat and wondered what was going on. She'd tried a couple of times last night to call Savannah, and again this morning, but her calls always went to voice mail. Seeing Kelly eased her anxiety a little bit. Since she'd given Savannah a ride home, at least she knew they weren't in an accident.

"Is she okay?" Maddie asked when she opened the door to let her inside.

"Yeah," Kelly answered with a wave of her hand. "She just has a bit of a headache from her injury. Plus, she doesn't have a four-wheel drive, so I don't know what she was thinking when she offered to pick you up today."

Maddie nodded, but it seemed Kelly was a little off. Like she was hiding something. Could Savannah be hurt more than she'd let on? She wanted to get home as soon as possible so she could see her for herself. She began getting her coat on, but her quick getaway was thwarted by Amy, who came bounding down the steps, probably expecting to see Savannah.

"Oh, my God, Kelly Rawlins is in my house!" she said, her eyes wide.

"Where?" Kelly asked, looking behind her. "Where is she?"

"You're her," Amy said, laughing. Maddie smiled. She had no idea Kelly had a playful side, and that she was so good with kids.

"Me?" Kelly placed a hand over her chest and looked at Amy. "Are you sure?"

"You're funny," Amy said, then looked at Maddie. "Maybe you should be dating her instead of Savannah."

"Savannah's funnier than I am," Kelly said seriously. "And I'm going to tell her you said that."

"No!" Amy looked horrified.

"We have to go," Maddie said to Amy. She gave her a hug then opened the front door after getting Duke on his leash. "Tell your mom I'll call her later, okay?"

"Sure." Amy turned and walked toward the kitchen.

They went to Kelly's truck without a word, and Maddie got Duke situated in the back seat. As Kelly began to drive, Maddie wanted to ask her what was really going on, but she wasn't sure how to phrase it. She didn't have to think too long about it though, because Kelly said something to make her even more suspicious.

"Listen, I think you should probably just let Savannah sleep today and not bother her until tomorrow."

"What?" Maddie turned in her seat so she could see Kelly better. "She's not okay, is she? Tell me what's going on."

Kelly clenched her teeth, causing the muscles in her jaw to twitch, and said nothing for a few moments. It was difficult, but Maddie forced herself to wait for her to speak.

"It isn't my place," she finally said, staring straight ahead.

"Kelly, please tell me what's wrong." Maddie hated begging for anything, but she wasn't sure how good Kelly was at keeping secrets. "I really care about her. I need to know."

"If you're really going back to Mary, then you should just forget about Savannah."

Maddie felt as though she'd been slapped. Her breath caught in her throat, and her vision turned a bit hazy. She shook her head and put a hand on Kelly's arm.

"What are you talking about?" she asked. "Mary cheated on me. I would never go back to her. Savannah knows this."

"Yeah, maybe she did before Mary ambushed her in the grocery store yesterday."

"What?" Maddie's pulse sped up, and she worried for a moment she might pass out. The feeling passed quickly as her anger took over. "She talked to Mary?"

Kelly told her what Mary had said to Savannah, and how Savannah had reacted to her news. She also told her the two of them had gotten drunk the night before, and how Savannah was on the verge of not wanting to see her ever again. Maddie swallowed the lump in her throat and had the very real urge to kill Mary. Almost a year after she'd blown up Maddie's life, and here she was trying to do it again. She'd mistakenly thought Mary left town because she hadn't heard from her since the night at her sister's.

How the hell had she even found out it was Savannah she was seeing? As soon as she'd asked herself the question she knew the answer though. Amy had given her all the information she'd needed to figure it out.

The game's on at eight tonight because the Warriors are in Chicago. Oh, and Aunt Maddie's girlfriend did not get suspended.

Christ, just a couple minutes on Google with that information and she would have easily come to the conclusion Savannah Wells was her girlfriend. Maddie couldn't believe she'd been so naïve to think Mary would have left town.

"It's all lies, Kelly," Maddie said, praying she'd believe her. But then again, it wasn't Kelly she needed to convince. "I did see her this week, and she said she wanted me back, but she doesn't really. She wants Duke. And she hates to lose. At anything."

"Then you aren't going to go back to her?" Kelly was still staring at the road ahead of her, and her jaw was twitching again.

"No, I already told you I wasn't." Maddie couldn't help but let the anger seep into her voice, and Kelly finally glanced at her.

"You can't get mad at Van when she asks you that, and you know she will."

"I'm sorry, and I know. I won't get mad at her."

"Do you love her?"

"I..." Maddie started to say she cared for her, but she thought about it for a moment. Why should she lie to Kelly? She knew she was falling for Savannah the night she paid the hockey rink owner to close the place to the public so Amy could skate with the Warriors. And every moment they spent together since, she fell even more for her. Yes, she loved Savannah, and although she knew Savannah should be the first one to hear those words, she also knew she needed to persuade Kelly too. "I do love her."

Kelly nodded, and Maddie thought she saw the hint of a smile on her lips.

"Good. Because I'm pretty sure she feels the same way." Kelly turned into Maddie's driveway but didn't cut the engine. She looked at Maddie. "But I still think you should give her some time. God, she's going to kill me when she finds out I told you all of this."

Maddie undid her seat belt and leaned over to kiss Kelly on the cheek. Kelly turned her head, but Maddie saw the blush on her cheeks.

"What was that for?" Kelly asked.

"Because you're a good friend," Maddie answered. She opened the door, but hesitated before getting out. "Thank you for telling me. And I promise, I won't let her kill you."

CHAPTER THIRTY-TWO

Savannah pulled the curtains open just enough to peek through and saw Kelly driving away. Movement caught her eye, and she saw Maddie walking to her own front door with Duke in tow. Her heart ached with the possibility she might never get to hold her in her arms again. To kiss her, to make love to her. All because of her own stupidity. She wouldn't be surprised if Maddie was pissed at her for her insecurities.

She groaned. Torturing herself wasn't getting her anywhere. This was exactly why getting involved with a neighbor wasn't a good idea. She let the curtains close and turned to find Leo sitting on the arm of the couch watching her intently. She scratched his chin as she walked by him.

"Don't judge me, little man," she said. "I'm an idiot, and I know it. It should have never gone beyond the fake dating."

She flopped down on the couch so Leo was now looking down at her. She covered her eyes with her arm and sighed. How had Maddie gotten past her walls? An even better question was why had she *allowed* Maddie to get past her walls? She'd known letting someone in again would only lead to heartbreak, yet with Maddie it hadn't seemed to matter. Now she was paying for her lapse in judgment.

Savannah opened her eyes when she heard a car outside and was surprised to see she'd slept for the past two hours. She pushed Leo off her chest and stood to look out the window. Her breath caught in her throat when she saw Mary getting out of a car in Maddie's driveway. She looked around the neighborhood briefly before walking to Maddie's front door.

Was it true then, the things Mary had told her? How else to explain Mary knowing where Maddie lived? She let the curtains fall closed and stalked to the kitchen to grab a beer. Now she was pissed as well as annoyed with herself. She'd almost convinced herself Mary had been lying to her, but it seemed now that perhaps she hadn't been.

❖

Maddie's heart jumped into her throat when she heard her doorbell ring. She was sure it had to be Savannah, and Duke thought so too. He followed her to the door, whining and wagging his tail the entire way. As soon as she opened the door though, his demeanor completely changed, as did hers. Duke took a step back and his hackles went up as he bared his teeth and let out a low growl. He never took his eyes off Mary. Maddie knew exactly how he felt.

"What the hell are you doing here?" she asked, making no move to let her enter the house. An even better question came to mind though. "How did you find out where I live?"

"It wasn't hard." Mary said with a shrug. "I waited at your sister's this morning and followed you home when that woman came to pick you up."

"You have a lot of nerve," Maddie said, her voice low. Duke obviously picked up on her mood, because his growling got louder and he stepped up to stand next to her. She looked down at him and wanted to praise him for his defense of her. She'd never seen him act this way before, and she was surprised at how intimidating he was. She placed a hand on top of his head and she felt him relax under her touch.

"Are you sleeping with that one too?" Mary asked, completely ignoring Duke.

"Who I may or may not be sleeping with is none of your business, Mary."

"Can I come in? It's cold out here."

"I don't think that would be a good idea," she said, glancing down at Duke. "We don't want you here."

"Hi, Duke," Mary said, finally looking at him. He snarled, and for a moment, Maddie feared he might lunge at Mary. She curled her fingers around his collar to hold him back. "How's my sweet boy? Do you want to come home with Mommy?"

"Are you insane? Do you see the way he's acting with you?" Maddie was incredulous. "Maybe you never truly noticed, but he obviously doesn't like you. Which is why I brought him here with me."

"Well, he's coming home with me." Mary looked her in the eye, and Maddie almost laughed out loud.

"You do realize he would probably attack you if I let go of him, right?"

"He would never attack me."

"Are you sure? Because right now, I'm not. He's never acted like this with anyone before. You really need to leave before I decide to release him if for no other reason than you deserve it for the lies you told Savannah."

"Oh, she told you?" Mary smiled sweetly, but Maddie knew she was angry. "I didn't lie to her. I want you to come back to Chicago with me. I thought if I told her you were, she'd make the decision easier for you."

"There's no decision to be made about it. Go home, Mary," Maddie said with a shake of her head. "Neither one of us is going anywhere with you. Ever. You left me, remember? I've moved on, and I suggest you do the same."

Maddie slammed the door in her face and took a deep breath. Mary knocked for a few minutes and pleaded with Maddie to let her in, but she didn't say a word. Mary eventually gave up, but Maddie didn't fully relax until she'd heard the car start and drive away. Duke was sitting in front her, staring up and panting. She dropped to her knees and held the sides of his head as she kissed him on the snout.

"You are such a good boy, Duke," she said, and he wagged his tail and licked her face happily. "Yes, you are."

❖

Savannah had no idea how long she stood there in the kitchen, but when her doorbell rang, she jumped. She set her beer down before heading to answer it. Her mistake was not looking to see who it was before opening the door.

"I need to talk to you," Maddie said as she walked past her, not even pretending to wait for an invitation. She took off her coat and faced Savannah, and that was when her face fell. She took a step toward Savannah and started to reach out to touch her cheek but pulled her hand back at the last second. "Oh my God, Savannah, your beautiful face."

"It looks worse than it is," Savannah said as she shut the door and led her into the living room. She didn't want Maddie here, but she wasn't one for throwing people out of her house. She stayed on her feet and watched Maddie as she sat on the couch. Leo, of course, climbed right onto her lap and curled up, staring at Savannah. *Traitor.* "Does Mary know you're here? She warned me to keep my distance."

"Will you please sit down. I don't want to have to crane my neck to speak to you." Maddie met her eyes and held her gaze, not backing down an inch. Savannah finally sat, but at the other end of the couch, as far away from Maddie as she could get. "So, you were spying on me?"

"I heard a car and thought it might have been in my driveway," Savannah said with a shrug. "I saw it was her and stopped looking."

"Well, if you'd kept watching, you would have seen she left only a few minutes later, and I never let her in the house."

"Really?" Savannah felt hope, but then she shook her head. "It doesn't matter."

"What do you mean it doesn't matter?" Maddie raised her voice, causing Leo to jump off her lap. "Everything she told you was a lie, Savannah. I would never go back to her. I don't have it in me to cheat on anyone, especially since I've been cheated on. I know how much it hurts, and I would never do that to anyone. I would never do it to *you*."

Savannah just looked at her in silence. Her pulse quickened as her mind began to ponder the impossible. Her heart stopped her train of thought though. She swallowed hard and forced herself not to look away from her.

"You didn't want me to go on this road trip."

"What?" Maddie looked truly puzzled by the statement.

"You said you wished I wasn't going."

"Because everything was so new between us. All I wanted was to spend every minute of every day in bed with you," Maddie said, softening her tone. "I'm not Shauna, Savannah. I know you're a hockey player, and I know you're a veterinarian. I would never hold either of those two things against you. Both of them are a huge part of you, and I love you because of them."

"Wait...what?" Savannah wasn't sure she heard her correctly. She was hoping she did, but she really needed to hear it again.

"Which part?" Maddie asked. The smile she gave was shy, yet seductive at the same time, and Savannah felt the warmth of it everywhere on her body.

"The last part." Savannah sat completely still as she waited, wanting to make sure she heard it right this time. Maddie nodded and moved closer to her as she reached for her hand.

"I love you." Maddie looked down at their hands in Savannah's lap. "I know it isn't what was supposed to happen, but it did. So, if you don't want to see me anymore, make it because of that instead of the lies Mary told you."

"I love you, too." Savannah smiled when Maddie's eyes snapped up to meet hers. "If I'm being honest, I knew it when you walked out of my bathroom wearing my jersey the first night we met. You rocked it so much better than I ever could."

"I knew it when you had the Warriors and Court Abbott skate with Amy." Maddie caressed her uninjured cheek. "You didn't have to do it, but it meant so much to Amy. To me, too."

"Do you think we have a chance to make this work?"

"I don't know, but I'm more than willing to give it a go if you are."

Savannah stood and held a hand out to her. Her arms slipped around Maddie's waist as she pulled their bodies flush. She kissed Maddie just below the ear then bit her earlobe lightly.

"I've missed you this past week," she murmured.

"Not nearly as much as I missed you," Maddie said. Savannah pulled back and looked into her eyes.

"Show me."

Maddie didn't wait for her to ask again. She pulled her down the hall into Savannah's bedroom and shut the door so Leo couldn't bother them.

"I intend to show you all night long," Maddie said, pulling Savannah's shirt over her head and tossing it to the side.

Savannah had always thought letting love into her heart again would be terrifying, but this felt more exhilarating than it did scary. She felt safe, and she felt loved. And she knew it had everything to do with the woman standing in front of her.

Chapter Thirty-three

Maddie opened her eyes and squinted at the sun shining in through the window before her. She tried to turn onto her back, but the warm body behind her prevented the move. Savannah's hand moved up her side and covered her breast. Maddie sighed and closed her eyes again.

"Good morning," Savannah said as she pressed her body firmly against hers and squeezed her breast gently.

"Good morning," Maddie replied. She pushed her ass back into Savannah and they both moaned quietly. "How long have you been awake?"

"Just a few minutes."

"You could have woken me up."

"I thought maybe I'd done that too many times through the night. I wanted to let you sleep."

"I don't remember complaining."

"Hmm," Savannah said as if she were contemplating. "No, I guess you didn't, did you?"

"I never would," Maddie said, turning onto her back and looking up at Savannah who was propping herself up on one elbow. She pressed a palm to Savannah's cheek. "I would never complain about you wanting to touch me."

"Good to know," Savannah said with a wink that threatened to melt Maddie's insides. Maddie sighed when Savannah looked down at her chest and began running her fingertips lightly over her stomach. "You are so beautiful. I can't imagine ever *not* wanting to touch you."

"Less talking, please," Maddie said, placing her hand on Savannah's hip and urging her on top of her. She spread her legs to give Savannah more room.

"I like the way you think," Savannah said with a wink before she closed her mouth around a nipple and sucked on it. Maddie's body surged and she was surprised to find she was ready to go again. She'd have thought after the night before she'd be well sated. It seemed she couldn't get enough of Savannah.

She placed her hands on Savannah's shoulders and urged her lower, which Savannah did without much prodding. Maddie moaned her pleasure when Savannah flicked her tongue across her clit, causing her body to jerk. Savannah's hands went to the insides of her thighs and spread her open farther before sliding two fingers inside her.

"More," Maddie said, a hint of desperation in her voice she hadn't heard before. "Jesus, Van, you feel so good."

Savannah readjusted and added a third finger before she took Maddie's clit between her lips and sucked as she thrust into her. Maddie felt herself tightening around her fingers just before the world exploded behind her eyes. She screamed her pleasure and arched her back off the bed as her body jerked.

"Stop, please," she whispered, her voice hoarse. Savannah chuckled as she slowly removed her fingers and then kissed her way back up Maddie's body, stopping when their lips met and she was fully on top of her, her hips nestled between Maddie's legs.

"Usually you aren't begging me to stop," she said into Maddie's ear.

"Usually you aren't stretching the capabilities of my body," Maddie answered with a sigh. "I think you've ruined me for other women."

"Good, because I don't like to share," Savannah said as she slid off her body and stretched out alongside her, one leg draped over Maddie's thighs.

"Why Savannah Wells, are you asking me to go steady?" Maddie joked.

"Yeah, I guess I am," Savannah said thoughtfully. "Too soon?"

"Not at all. I don't like to share either."

"Good." She grinned when she remembered what Maddie had called her a few moments earlier.

"What?" Maddie asked, looking into her eyes.

"You called me Van."

"Did I?" Maddie looked surprised but then smiled. "Do you mind?"

"Not at all. Just don't call me Vanna."

Savannah felt lighter than she had in what seemed like forever when she took the ice for their first game of a crucial home stand a couple of days later. Things were awesome with Maddie, and Mary had returned to Chicago, hopefully to leave them alone for good.

"When's the wedding?" Kelly asked when they were standing at center ice waiting for the national anthem to start.

"Wedding?" Savannah asked with a laugh. "Don't rush me."

"Why not? First Court, and now you." Kelly shrugged. "Seems like everybody around me is coupling up. A wedding seems the next logical step, doesn't it?"

"You sound upset," Savannah said when the anthem was done and they were at the bench waiting to get ready for the opening face-off.

"Nah," Kelly said with a light whack of her stick to her shins. "I'm happy for you. Maybe someday I'll find a good woman to settle down with."

"I hope you do," Savannah said with a nod. They skated to center ice and Alex got ready for the puck to drop. Savannah glanced up at the seats behind their bench and saw Maddie smiling at her. She couldn't help but smile back.

They won the game 8-2, and Savannah had three goals and four assists, the best offensive game of her career. She was so happy she didn't even let Hilton's jabs get to her. That didn't mean Hilton didn't try though.

"You could have let the rest of us get some points tonight, you know," Hilton said as she passed her on the way to her locker.

"Nobody stopped the rest of you from joining in," Savannah said with a chuckle. "Well, except for the other team."

Kelly laughed and gave her an elbow to the side. Savannah could see Hilton stopped in her tracks and was facing them. She nudged Kelly and shook her head to get her to stop laughing. It didn't much matter though, because the rest of the team had already joined in, including Hilton's line mates.

"You think you're so much better than the rest of us," Hilton said, starting to come back their way. Charlotte Green, their goalie, stepped in her path. Hilton looked up at her, because Charlotte was a good six inches taller than she was.

"We won the damn game, Hilton," she said. "Be happy for once in your life."

"Fuck off," Hilton said and tried to step around her. Charlotte's hand to her biceps stopped her. "Let go of me."

"Why are you always so pissed off?" Charlotte asked. "And nobody in this locker room is better than anyone else. I'm just so tired of listening to your shit and putting up with your drama every freaking day. Enjoy the win like the rest of us are doing, and save your bullshit for another time, okay?"

Hilton stared at her for a moment before jerking her arm away from her and stalking off to her own locker. Savannah felt the collective sigh from everyone in the room, Gail included. She was standing a few feet away watching intently. When it was over, Gail looked at Savannah and smiled with a nod.

Maddie was waiting for Savannah outside the locker room with Dana, Amy, and Trent. Savannah smiled and went right to her to give her a quick kiss on the cheek.

"Is that all I get?" Maddie asked with a pout.

"For now," Savannah said. "I'll make up for it later."

They all walked to the parking lot together, but split up when they reached Trent's car first. Savannah hung back while Maddie said her good-byes, and they joined hands when they headed for Savannah's car a couple of rows over.

"You seem quiet tonight," Maddie said.

"Do I? I was just thinking."

"About what?"

"Something Kelly said to me earlier tonight." Savannah's heart was pounding so hard she thought for certain Maddie must have heard it. She stopped walking and took a deep breath. Maddie looked at her, the concern evident in her eyes. Savannah smiled at her. She hadn't given much thought to it before tonight, but since Kelly had mentioned it, she couldn't seem to think of a good reason for it not to happen. She just hoped Maddie felt the same.

"You're worrying me, Savannah. What's going on?"

"Have you ever thought about getting married?" Savannah cringed at the words, knowing she was botching this big time.

"Maybe," Maddie said hesitantly as she tilted her head to the side.

"Never mind," Savannah shook her head and started walking again, but Maddie grabbed her hand and gave it a tug, causing her to turn and face her again.

"You can't ask that question out of the blue and then just walk away," Maddie said with a shake of her head. "Are you trying to propose to me?"

"Maybe," Savannah said as hesitantly as Maddie had a moment earlier. "I guess it depends on what your answer is."

"So, if I said no, then this would not be a proposal?" Maddie laughed. "And if I said yes it would be?"

"I don't have a ring to give you, so I guess either way it would not be a proposal." Savannah sighed and wished she'd thought this through more completely before even bringing it up. She tried to walk toward her car again, but once more Maddie stopped her.

"Then maybe I should do it."

Savannah stared at her in disbelief as Maddie got down on one knee. She checked their surroundings to see if anyone was watching, but the parking lot was mostly empty this long after the game had finished. She felt her cheeks flush as she watched Maddie pull a small box out of her coat pocket.

"Maddie, what are you doing?"

"I'm doing what you were trying to do, only I'm doing it better," Maddie said, smiling, as she opened the box to reveal a simple gold band. "Savannah Wells, will you marry me?"

Savannah's throat constricted and she wasn't sure she could speak. Was this really happening? Two weeks ago, she would have laughed in Maddie's face for even suggesting this, but now? She couldn't think of any reason to say anything but yes. Maddie had so completely captured her heart she knew living without her would destroy her. She nodded emphatically as she felt tears rolling down her cheeks.

"Yes?" Maddie asked, getting back to her feet. "Are you saying yes?"

"Yes," she finally managed to say. Maddie slid the ring on her finger before enveloping her in a hug so tight Savannah could hardly breathe. She pulled back and looked in Maddie's eyes as the hug loosened. "I love you, Madison Scott."

"That's good to know, because I would hate to think I'm marrying someone who doesn't love me."

They kissed then, and Savannah had never been so happy. She tried to convey in this kiss what she was getting from Maddie—the promise of love and devotion. The promise of everlasting passion. And the promise of a happily ever after.

About the Author

PJ Trebelhorn was born and raised in the greater metropolitan area of Portland, Oregon. Her love of sports (mainly baseball and ice hockey) was fueled in part by her father's interests. She likes to brag about the fact that her uncle managed the Milwaukee Brewers for five years and the Chicago Cubs for one year.

PJ now resides in western New York with her wife, Cheryl, their three cats and one very neurotic dog. When not writing or reading, PJ enjoys watching movies, playing on the Playstation, and spending way too much time with stupid games on Facebook. After living in the Philadelphia area for nearly twenty years, she still roots for the Flyers, Phillies, and Eagles, even though she's now in Sabres and Bills territory.

Books Available from Bold Strokes Books

Date Night by Raven Sky. Quinn and Riley are celebrating their one-year anniversary. Such an important milestone is bound to result in some extraordinary sexual adventures, but precisely how extraordinary is up to you, dear reader. (978-1-63555-655-1)

Face Off by PJ Trebelhorn. Hockey player Savannah Wells rarely spends more than a night with any one woman, but when photographer Madison Scott buys the house next door, she's forced to rethink what she expects out of life. (978-1-63555-480-9)

Hot Ice by Aurora Rey, Elle Spencer, Erin Zak. Can falling in love melt the hearts of the iciest ice queens? Join Aurora Rey, Elle Spencer, and Erin Zak to find out! (978-1-63555-513-4)

Line of Duty by VK Powell. Dr. Dylan Carlyle's professional and personal life is turned upside down when a tragic event at Fairview Station pits her against ambitious, handsome police officer Finley Masters. (978-1-63555-486-1)

London Undone by Nan Higgins. London Craft reinvents her life after reading a childhood letter to her future self and in doing so finds the love she truly wants. (978-1-63555-562-2)

Lunar Eclipse by Gun Brooke. Moon De Cruz lives alone on an uninhabited planet after being shipwrecked in space. Her life changes forever when Captain Beaux Lestarion's arrival threatens the planet and Moon's freedom. (978-1-63555-460-1)

One Small Step by Michelle Binfield. Iris and Cam discover the meaning of taking chances and following your heart, even if it means getting hurt. (978-1-63555-596-7)

Shadows of a Dream by Nicole Disney. Rainn has the talent to take her rock band all the way, but falling in love is a powerful distraction, and her new girlfriend's meth addiction might just take them both down. (978-1-63555-598-1)

Someone to Love by Jenny Frame. When Davina Trent is given an unexpected family, can she let nanny Wendy Darling teach her to open her heart to the children and to Wendy? (978-1-63555-468-7)

Tinsel by Kris Bryant. Did a sweet kitten show up to help Jessica Raymond and Taylor Mitchell find each other? Or is the holiday spirit to blame for their special connection? (978-1-63555-641-4)

Uncharted by Robyn Nyx. As Rayne Marcellus and Chase Stinsen track the legendary Golden Trinity, they must learn to put their differences aside and depend on one another to survive. (978-1-63555-325-3)

Where We Are by Annie McDonald. Can two women discover a way to walk on the same path together and discover the gift of staying in one spot, in time, in space, and in love? (978-1-63555-581-3)

A Moment in Time by Lisa Moreau. A longstanding family feud separates two women who unexpectedly fall in love at an antique clock shop in a small Louisiana town. (978-1-63555-419-9)

Aspen in Moonlight by Kelly Wacker. When art historian Melissa Warren meets Sula Johansen, director of a local bear conservancy, she discovers that love can come in unexpected and unusual forms. (978-1-63555-470-0)

Back to September by Melissa Brayden. Small bookshop owner Hannah Shepard and famous romance novelist Parker Bristow maneuver the landscape of their two very different worlds to find out if love can win out in the end. (978-1-63555-576-9)

Changing Course by Brey Willows. When the woman of your dreams falls from the sky, you'd better be ready to catch her. (978-1-63555-335-2)

Cost of Honor by Radclyffe. First Daughter Blair Powell and Homeland Security Director Cameron Roberts face adversity when their enemies stop at nothing to prevent President Andrew Powell's reelection. (978-1-63555-582-0)

Fearless by Tina Michele. Determined to overcome her debilitating fear through exposure therapy, Laura Carter all but fails before she's even begun until dolphin trainer Jillian Marshall dedicates herself to helping Laura defeat the nightmares of her past. (978-1-63555-495-3)

Not Dead Enough by J.M. Redmann. A woman who may or may not be dead drags Micky Knight into a messy con game. (978-1-63555-543-1)

Not Since You by Fiona Riley. When Charlotte boards her honeymoon cruise single and comes face-to-face with Lexi, the high school love she left behind, she questions every decision she has ever made. (978-1-63555-474-8)

Not Your Average Love Spell by Barbara Ann Wright. Four women struggle with who to love and who to hate while fighting to rid a kingdom of an evil invading force. (978-1-63555-327-7)

Tennessee Whiskey by Donna K. Ford. Dane Foster wants to put her life on pause and ask for a redo, a chance for something that matters. Emma Reynolds is that chance. (978-1-63555-556-1)

30 Dates in 30 Days by Elle Spencer. A busy lawyer tries to find love the fast way—thirty dates in thirty days. (978-1-63555-498-4)

Finding Sky by Cass Sellars. Skylar Addison's search for a career intersects with her new boss's search for butterflies, but Skylar can't forgive Jess's intrusion into her life. (978-1-63555-521-9)

Hammers, Strings, and Beautiful Things by Morgan Lee Miller. While on tour with the biggest pop star in the world, rising musician Blair Bennett falls in love for the first time while coping with loss and depression. (978-1-63555-538-7)

Heart of a Killer by Yolanda Wallace. Contract killer Santana Masters's only interest is her next assignment—until a chance meeting with a beautiful stranger tempts her to change her ways. (978-1-63555-547-9)

Leading the Witness by Carsen Taite. When defense attorney Catherine Landauer reluctantly becomes the key witness in prosecutor Starr Rio's latest criminal trial, their hearts, careers, and lives may be at risk. (978-1-63555-512-7)

No Experience Required by Kimberly Cooper Griffin. Izzy Treadway has resigned herself to a life without romance because of her bipolar illness but wonders what she's gotten herself into when she agrees to write a book about love. (978-1-63555-561-5)

One Walk in Winter by Georgia Beers. Olivia Santini and Hayley Boyd Markham might be rivals at work, but they discover that lonely hearts often find company in the most unexpected of places. (978-1-63555-541-7)

The Inn at Netherfield Green by Aurora Rey. Advertising executive Lauren Montgomery and gin distiller Camden Crawley don't agree on anything except saving the Rose & Crown, the old English pub that's brought them together. (978-1-63555-445-8)

Top of Her Game by M. Ullrich. When it comes to life on the field and matters of the heart, losing isn't an option for pro athletes Kenzie Shaw and Sutton Flores. (978-1-63555-500-4)

Vanished by Eden Darry. A storm is coming, and Ellery and Loveday must find the chosen one or humanity won't survive it. (978-1-63555-437-3)

All She Wants by Larkin Rose. Marci Jones and Tessa Dalton get more than they bargained for when their plans for a one-night stand turn into an opportunity for love. (978-1-63555-476-2)

Beautiful Accidents by Erin Zak. Stevie Adams and Bernadette Thompson discover that sometimes the best things in life happen purely by accident. (978-1-63555-497-7)

Before Now by Joy Argento. Can Delany and Jade overcome the betrayal that spans the centuries to reignite a love that can't be broken? (978-1-63555-525-7)

Breathe by Carl Hunter. Paramedic Jemima Pardon's chronic bad luck seems to be improving when she meets police officer Rosie Jones. But they face a battle to survive before they can find love. (978-1-63555-523-3)

Double-Crossed by Ali Vali. Hired thief and killer Reed Gable finds something in her scope that will change her life forever when she gets a contract to end casino accountant Brinley Myers's life. (978-1-63555-302-4)

False Horizons by CJ Birch. Jordan and Ash struggle with different views on the alien agenda and must find their way back to each other before they're swallowed up by a centuries-old war. (978-1-63555-519-6)

Legacy by Charlotte Greene. When five women hike to a remote cabin deep inside a national park, unsettling events suggest that they should have stayed home. (978-1-63555-490-8)

Royal Street Reveillon by Greg Herren. Someone is killing the stars of a reality show, and it's up to Scotty Bradley and the boys to find out who. (978-1-63555-545-5)

Somewhere Along the Way by Kathleen Knowles. When Maxine Cooper moves to San Francisco during the summer of 1981, she learns that wherever you run, you cannot escape yourself. (978-1-63555-383-3)

Blood of the Pack by Jenny Frame. When Alpha of the Scottish pack Kenrick Wulver visits the Wolfgangs, she falls for Zaria Lupa, a wolf on the run. (978-1-63555-431-1)

Cause of Death by Sheri Lewis Wohl. Medical student Vi Akiak and K9 Search and Rescue officer Kate Renard must work together to find a killer before they end up the next targets. In the race for survival, they discover that love may be the biggest risk of all. (978-1-63555-441-0)

Chasing Sunset by Missouri Vaun. Hijinks and mishaps ensue as Iris and Finn set off on a road trip adventure, chasing the sunset, and falling in love along the way. (978-1-63555-454-0)

Double Down by MB Austin. When an unlikely friendship with Spanish pop star Erlea turns deeper, Celeste, in-house physician for the hotel hosting Erlea's show, has a choice to make—run or double down on love. (978-1-63555-423-6)

Party of Three by Sandy Lowe. Three friends are in for a wild night at billionaire heiress Eleanor McGregor's twenty-fifth birthday party. Love, lust, and doing the right thing, even when it hurts, turn the evening into one that will change their lives forever. (978-1-63555-246-1)

Sit. Stay. Love. by Karis Walsh. City girl Alana Brendt and country vet Tegan Evans both know they don't belong together. Only problem is, they're falling in love. (978-1-63555-439-7)

Where the Lies Hide by Renee Roman. As P.I. Camdyn Stark gets closer to solving the case, will her dark secrets and the lies she's buried jeopardize her future with the quietly beautiful Sarah Peters? (978-1-63555-371-0)